I0684918

Damsels of June

Kira Vorobiyova

Arizona USA

Damsels of June

Copyright © 2014 by Cactus Rain Publishing
Copyright actively enforced.

First Edition.

Damsels of June is a work of fiction. Names, characters, places, and incidents are fictitious or are used fictitiously. Any perceived resemblance to actual persons, living or dead, business establishments, events, or locales is false.

Published by Cactus Rain Publishing, LLC
San Tan Valley, Arizona, USA
www.CactusRainPublishing.com

ISBN 978-0-9829181-4-2

Cover Design by Laura Mitchell

Published June 1, 2014
Printed in the United States of America

For the city of Kiev,
its faithful dwellers,
and the stirring memories of youth
they etched upon my heart.

Kira Vorobiyova

Damsels of June

Kira Vorobiyova

Prologue

The air in the train station was stiff, permeated with the stench of cigarettes, beer, cheap perfume, and male sweat. It was mid-May, but the temperatures were those of a blistering August afternoon.

At half past four, a hasty announcement was made over the loudspeakers.

"Attention! Warsaw-bound passenger train 119 will be ready for boarding shortly. Please, make your way to platform five."

This was the third in a series of similar announcements made over the course of the hour, and the people, having been falsely excited before, were now wary of any such proclamation. Many remained seated, shifting uncomfortably on the steel benches, their skin stuck to the worn, thin lining of artificial burgundy leather coating the backrests. Everyone waited for someone else to rise first and take the lead as if assuming responsibility for the entire group somehow authenticated the promised arrival of the train.

"Attention! The ticketing window is now closed. All sales are final. Those seeing off their parties are forbidden to enter the cars. Passengers, please proceed to platform 5 immediately," echoed the grating voice through the waiting hall. Because it was a passing train, having begun its journey in Moscow, boarding would have to be swift and farewells cut short.

Dessa jumped up and protracted her arms toward the high concave ceiling. It held two heavy, pear-shaped chandeliers she predicted would sparkle in the sunlight streaming from the fixed clerestory windows, but they were marred by a dense mass of dust hanging above them like a storm cloud. A thin film of perspiration still lingered on the edge of her seat. Unlike the rest, she had no scruples about taking charge of the group. It was a matter of necessity, she thought, and imagined herself as an officer in command of an elite military unit.

Tugging on her mother's blouse, Dessa motioned toward the escalators. The woman waved her off indifferently, pulled a crumpled, silk handkerchief out of her skirt pocket, tilted her head forward, and wiped the glistening beads of sweat gathered at the nape of her neck. She could have done without the girl; there were relatives, who expressed interest in taking her, but Chuck insisted she come with them, and there was no use dissuading him. For reasons inexplicable to her, he came to love this petulant child as his own and would not hear of leaving her behind as they embarked on their great journey to America.

Grabbing her knapsack, Dessa stood erect, scanned the hall with an air of sophistication, turned on her heels and, authoritatively marched to the escalator. She expected a chain reaction to take place behind her; for men, women, and children to stir in unison and follow obediently. On the contrary, heads bobbed, bodies bent, feet scuffled, and clammy palms grasped at oversized luggage in a coordinated dance of chaos.

The train came to a full stop with a reassuring hiss just as Dessa stepped onto the open platform. Cigarette butts coated the ground, whilst the designated receptacles stood empty. The smell of tobacco was stronger than ever, with a rush of fresh air turning the foul odour into an enchanting fragrance. She evoked memories of old Hollywood sirens and their lovers she caught glimpses of on the late-night telly where every frame was saturated with the pearly haze of smoke, imagining it must have smelled something like this.

The rest of the group now piled onto the platform, and she was reunited with her mother and Chuck, who clutched Dessa by the elbows on either side and steered her toward one of the cars, flinging her past the conductor and up the steps. Dessa entered the coach while the grown-ups trailed behind, sorting out the tickets.

Traversing the deserted, narrow hallway, she read the cabin numbers out loud before stopping abruptly in front of the only one with a cracked door. She slid it open, revealing an empty four-berth sleeper that they would have to themselves for the next day or so. It was Chuck's treat, flexing his wallet to buy out the cabin in order to impress Mother.

Dessa looked forward to having free reign of the upper bunks, drowning in the darkness above everyone else as the rhythmic vibrations of a train lulled her to sleep. She heard voices in the hall and sat on the right-hand bunk. It was pleasantly cool. Without success, she stretched out her legs to see if her toes would reach the other side. She scooted toward the window as Mother and Chuck crowded into the sleeper, pushing larger suitcases under the bunks and placing the rest on the seats. There was something decidedly crass in their frenzy. Not wanting to be disturbed by them, Dessa climbed on the top bunk, observing a stack of white linen crowned with a thick goose down pillow. She lowered her head and took a deep breath. The sheets smelled freshly pressed and were crisp to the touch.

In a matter of moments once the train departed, the chronic unpleasantness of events that unfolded months prior would be all but forgotten. The soothing jolt came, and the platform, with its sea of smiles, tears and waving handkerchiefs, glided smoothly past their window. Dessa closed her eyes and swallowed hard.

She reached into her knapsack and took out an envelope. Inside was an outdated pocket calendar. She rotated it between her fingers and brought it closer, catching a faint whiff of rose water once spilled on it by accident. She could not remember if it were Klara or Inna who caused the spill. It did not quite matter. This negligible piece of cardstock was the last evidence left of them, of their time together, and of their eventual tragedy. It was her common practice to recall the photograph with eyes closed, conjuring the all-too-familiar image, then lifting the self-imposed blindfold to confirm her memory of three young girls resting on a cream-coloured chaise longue with their backs to the camera and their faces in profile. With shoulders bare, feet drawn under, arms intertwined, all but one looked somewhere beyond the range of the apparatus.

The bold one, without any shyness or shame, her piercing gaze steady and unapologetic, was Dessa.

Chapter 1

It was a typical Tuesday in the summer of '91. The city of Kiev bustled with people and activity at a time of day when everyone walked with a purpose, clicking their heels, clutching their purses and briefcases. For ten-year-old Dessa Faustova, it was a rare opportunity to enjoy people in the prime of their day. In the early hours of the afternoon, everyone was still gussied up. Women strutted confidently, swaying their hips and stroking their hair as passing men countered with perked-up chins and straightened postures, catching a skip in their step.

In a matter of hours, everything would change. After five o'clock, heels no longer clicked, they dragged, as tired women made their way home from work, wavering unevenly on their feet. Some had runs in their stockings and dishevelled hair, their faces caricatured by faded lipstick, creased eyeliner, and smeared rouge. Men stumbled along with ties loosened, belt buckles twisted off centre, their shirts no longer crisp, fresh, or tucked flawlessly in their trousers. Congregating at trolley stops and metro platforms, they reached into pockets for wrinkled handkerchiefs to wipe the beads of sweat running down their foreheads.

Aware of having exhausted much time watching people, Dessa rushed down the unevenly paved Chkalov Street, preparing to cut through a neighbouring courtyard in hopes of making her two o'clock piano lesson on time.

Mother was at work and, for the first time in years, had no available friends or sitters on call to keep the girl company. That very morning, it was decided Dessa was old enough to walk the familiar route on her own. The lessons were held only several blocks away and did not require the use of a public transport. The area was often referenced as the intellectual district of Kiev because its radius was packed with historical landmarks, fine opera houses, ballet schools, musical conservatories, and golden-domed cathedrals, including an array of museums to satisfy even the most curious whim. Many of the residents in surrounding buildings were employees of these cultural establishments, and it was widely regarded that no real harm could possibly come to a child in the civilized, upper-crust community.

As she crossed the courtyard, inhaling the fragrance of blooming linden trees, Dessa felt a peculiar sense of urgency in the air. It was not because of her perpetual lateness, or her fear of not having practised enough before the lesson. She felt this urgency was on a much larger, almost national scale. Something big was brewing, a change of vast proportions, but she was unsure of what it was or how it would affect her personally, if at all. There were times, particularly during nightly tea, that hushed whispers carried through the open windows of kitchens above and below.

For Dessa, the intrigue lay in the whisper itself, rather than its content. There was talk of change that came with perestroika, except no one fathomed something as radical as a declaration of independence. Admittedly, the concept of autonomy was much too inclusive for the young girl to grasp.

What it entailed for the nation did not matter a great deal in comparison to possible personal gain. Would her curfew change? Would the strict diet of rye biscuits and seasonal fruit enlisted by Mother be lifted? What about the stringency and length of her punishments? Was there any guarantee that this highly sought-after independence would spare her from what she thought to be a wretched existence?

She hurried toward the main entrance of a drab five-story building and jammed a worn buzzer next to a partially faded name. Within seconds, the hatches clicked, and the girl disappeared into the cool, musty darkness, her footsteps echoing on the concrete stairs. Like most in the area, this apartment complex was a remnant of the Stalinist design of stucco over simple brick masonry, but had not been renovated since its construction in the late forties. The rosewood-hued bricks peeked through in patches under the chipping boulder-grey stucco, a ghastly contrast that roused images of blood seeping through decaying scraps of flesh. On the inside, the complex lacked an elevator, a meagre inconvenience for visitors turned into a permanent handicap for most of the older occupants. The winding staircase was unusually dark, and not even the most powerful, brightly lit bulb could illuminate the seemingly endless corridors that branched out from every subsequent landing.

Dessa sprinted to the fourth floor and, upon entering the corridor, noticed that the front door of Lady Ramazanova's flat was already ajar. The subtle act was her way of acknowledging the girl's tardiness; one that she had hoped would, over time, eradicate the unbecoming behaviour. Dessa was more than aware of the woman's passive- aggressive nature and thought it a wicked pleasure to arrive a few minutes late. She swore that had Lady Ramazanova asked her nicely to be prompt, she would be. In fact, had she asked Dessa to do anything nicely, the girl would have readily obliged. It was the petty game of few words and contrived actions that drove the youngster absolutely mad. Lady Rama, as the pupils called her, was in her early forties and utterly alone. She was the subject of never-ending prattle in the courtyard, a woman who had failed at being a woman, a mother, or a lover. Her face was rooted in a permanent frown with an acute self-awareness of her shortcomings. There were instances ever so brief when Dessa felt genuine concern, yet the woman's unwelcoming, trivial nature made it difficult to sustain consistent sympathy.

"Life dealt that one a bad hand," hissed the gossiping snakes whenever she dared show her face in public. Whether or not this was the case became less and less clear to the young girl, who believed that the only destiny people were bound to face was death. Everything else was a choice that would either get one a step closer to or a step farther from their desires. If this were Lady Rama's life, then she thought it necessary to live in isolation, perhaps as a form of penance for something yet unknown.

Crossing the cramped foyer into the common room, Dessa noted a slight change in surroundings from her last visit. There was an unfamiliar pair of moccasins below the coat rack that didn't appear to belong. They looked worn, too generous in size for Rama, and Dessa was the lone pupil there. Intrigued, she paused to give them another look, spying fresh water stains on the tan leather. It had not rained in weeks.

"Shall we get started? You certainly aren't the last today," snapped a coarse voice from the parlour.

Dessa bounced inside without a glance in Rama's direction in the far corner of the room. She scooted swiftly onto the creaky piano bench and placed a stack of crumpled sheet music in front of her. With a deep breath and a theatrical sway of the arms, she stroked the keys, bringing Schubert's "Serenade" to life. It was a sensation like no other. Her Grandpapa Shurik, a concert

4

pianist of five decades, had told her that to be left alone in a room with Schubert was to witness a magnificent aura of togetherness. "You were together with his kindness, his peace, and his love for nature."

Except, she was not alone. Rama's penetrating stare twisted in disapproval. Her body was stiff, her breaths short, calculated, and cold. She tapped her heel on the floor as if to establish a pace, but Dessa kept on. Fermata, staccato, tenuto, largo, andante, moderato, presto, flats, sharps, majors, minors, whole notes and eighth notes were all markings on a page that held no immediate meaning to Dessa. Although the definitions were ingrained in her mind, there was no way to tap the source for practical application. Instead, she relied on raw memories of Grandpapa's recitals, bearing witness to the overwhelming veneration of opera house patrons as he bewitched them with his musical sorcery.

"Head up! You must follow the text."

"I know it by heart."

"Ungracious child! Who shall take you seriously when you can't read your sheet music?"

Lady Rama rushed over and waved the girl off, taking her place on the piano bench. She tugged at her shawl, rubbed her palms together, cleared her throat, and began to play.

Dessa squeezed her fists tightly. There was nothing especially enticing about Rama's ability. She was mediocre at best, able to work because of her contacts at the Conservatory. Everything about her was average; her looks, her talent, her flat, even her Soviet-made upright Lira was nowhere near the decadent baby grand Ibach or the nine-foot Blüthner Dessa was spoiled with at home.

Were it up to her, she would learn the craft exclusively from her beloved Shurik, who was so engaged with concerts that what spare time they did share together was spent in his library

5

flipping through Parisian art books and reciting poetry. On rare occasions she requested he play for her with free reign over composers and their works. This was where she took note of the compositions' proper dynamics and tempo. After having heard it once, she was keenly aware of the work that had to be done in order to recreate his performance. It was the only way she was able to approach the material, and while most reckoned it to be a curious gift, Lady Rama called attention to Dessa's supposed inferiority. She thought playing by ear to be an unambitious pastime and would not indulge the girl in her method.

"Go on then, from the top and all the way through," she said, scooting to the edge of the bench and patting the place by her side. Dessa took her spot and gently brushed the keys with her fingertips. She focussed on the papers saturated with infinite black dots, watching them come to life. The notes bounced from staff to staff, the clefs switched places, flats became sharps and sharps became neutrals. None of it made any sense. She gave it a go. What she heard was a sound of discord followed by another and then another. Her palms were sweating, and Rama's unforgiving glare felt as if a handful of scorching coals were about to be thrust against her skin.

This feeling of panic and helplessness, however, was no foreign phenomenon. Aware of an imminent blackout, the girl braced herself. She would come to in the comfort of her own bed, with the lesson at Lady Rama's a distant memory. The adults would be temporarily softened with worry, a perfect opportunity to plead for a better instructor, one that could readily embrace her talent or, at the very least, skillfully masquerade their resentment. Much would be made of the plea for a good hour or two, and with no feasible solution in sight, they would concur for everything to stay as is. With a shock of warmth in her chest and lightness in her extremities, she gave way to the darkness.

Chapter 2

The massive steel doors of Streletzkaya's apartment building swung open, and Dessa emerged hand in hand with her dearest friend Klara Feldblum. Skipping side by side, both were equally awkward in appearance, long legged, and exceptionally thin. Fridays were characteristic of great mischief and adventure, but before any real fun could be had, a ballet practice at the Opera House was in order.

The dance program was part of a specialised curriculum at the Braga Lyceum, an exclusive school for gifted children. Dessa was enrolled because of advanced reading skills and foreign language comprehension. Her subsequent progression was so rapid, that the committee was inclined to fast track her through several grades, making her the lone ten-year-old among adolescents.

Klara attended a regular school that basked in an aura of prestige because of its geographic proximity to the city's cultural centre. Her older brother Yakov worked as a cataloguing apprentice at Braga Lyceum's Bibliotheca, a privilege that afforded him the opportunity to register his baby sister in an otherwise impenetrable ballet academy.

Although Klara was the same age, she studied in the fifth grade like most without special advances and crossed school paths with Dessa only within the bounds of the Opera House and only on Fridays when all levels were collectively taught as one. Braga's program required daily attendance, whereas Klara's enrollment involved a mere two classes per week.

Dessa's mother was not keen on this attachment, but the girls met years ago on the swings of their courtyard, and after realizing they lived just two floors apart, their friendship was signed and sealed.

The singular reason for Mother's dislike originated from an early awareness that Klara came from a dynasty of Russian Jews. Even in appearance, her stock, thick black curls, bushy brows, and prominent facial features clearly pointed at her Jewishness. Despite being the offspring of intellectuals, her family was inherently poor or, rather, poorer than most. While their academic status was the stroke of good fortune that granted access to a lavish apartment in the iconic sector of the city, the lingering prejudice did not garner them any significant acquaintanceships.

Dessa failed to understand the distrust with which many viewed the Feldblums. True poverty was on the back streets, in metro underpasses, and abandoned courtyards where persons slept under heaps of dailies and sat on the steps of bakeries at dawn, begging for a scrap to be thrown their way. Here, the Feldblums' modesty was deliberately perceived as hardship.

The unfavourable sentiments further bred Dessa's animosity toward her flamboyant mother and a rotten gambling uncle; both flagrantly claimed and flaunted an empire of wealth they did not lift a finger to earn. In a state built on the fundamental belief of a classless and moneyless social order, everyone was suddenly preoccupied with shaming modesty in lieu of opulence. The tide was turning.

The avenues were curiously jammed with traffic, and the sidewalks provided little relief as hordes of people poured out of the busy Golden Gates metro station. The girls slipped into a labyrinth of back alleys and courtyards to cut through the chaos. Within minutes, they were facing a private entrance in the west wing of the Opera House.

Inside, they passed through spacious, boundless corridors covered in rainbows of tulle. Because this was also the costumier wing, breathtaking tutus hung on the walls as seamstresses stitched, threaded,, embroidered and mended in their adjoining chambers. It was a marvellous game to guess the figures and ballets to which the costumes belonged. Odettes, Odiles, and Auroras wore the platter skirts. The ever-ethereal Giselle with her corps de ballet claimed the romantic tutus. The ruby-red bell skirts belonged to the fiery Carmens, Paquitas, and Kitris.

Dessa craved the day when she could be fitted in one of these delicate creations as a prima ballerina taking the stage in a spectacular solo performance. She imagined the patrons intoxicated by her grace as they peered through their opera glasses with gasps of awe. She felt the synchronized bows from the backdrop corps, saw the winks and nods from the orchestra pit, inhaled the heaps of roses and chrysanthemums tossed on stage, heard the infinite standing ovations peppered with bravos and encores; a vision so sensational, it could not possibly ring true. Picking up the pace and spreading her arms, she brushed her fingertips through the fabric as she moved along, savouring a rare moment of genuine pleasure.

At the end of the hall, a line of fifty or so pupils had already formed. Everyone was eager to step inside and stretch before Mistress Galina made her grand entrance. The consensus of the group was that she appeared less strict in collective rehearsals, but was unbearably demanding in the specialized courses that Dessa also had to attend.

At last, the double doors swung open, and a scrawny young man motioned for the girls to come in. He was the ballet pianist. The studio smelled fresh. They were the first students of the day. Everyone quickly huddled around the rosin boxes, frantically stepping in with one pointe and then the other. Without a moment to waste, the girls went straight to the barre extending all the way around the studio and began to warm up their muscles. Some fiddled with their chignons, others fixed their leotards. There was hardly chatter, as all were consumed with preparation. The sound of pointes gliding along the massive hardwood floor was in full effect. Discipline reigned.

In the distance, a door opened and slammed shut. After a slight pause, calculated footsteps echoed throughout the hallway. They were sharp, restrained, and severe. Click, clock. Click, clock. The strides were soon accentuated by a tyrannical jab of her cane. Within seconds, Mistress Galina would enter and commence Friday's rehearsal. An air of panic swept the studio as trembling bodies raced to form a straight line at the barre and fidgeted in place to assume first position. Their feet aligned perfectly heel-to-heel, right arms in bras bas, torsos pulled in, necks elongated, and heads held high, the pupils awaited further instruction.

"Fifty pliés! From the top, Sasha!" barked the Mistress turning in the doorway.

The young man squirmed on the bench and, with a terse grunt, introduced a variation of intermezzo from Cavalleria Rusticana. In perfect unison, knees bent just below the hips and reverted smoothly to their starting positions.

Mistress Galina made the rounds, scrutinizing every limb, tracking every faint breath. Her exterior was as austere as her disposition. A woman of about sixty, she owned a limited wardrobe of black calf-length skirts and Victorian cream-coloured blouses accented by a string of graduated pearls. Her lips were carved in a thin red line, her auburn hair fixed in a Marcel wave. She alternated between two pairs of moderately heeled shoes, either the grey t-strap pumps or worn-out beige oxfords. Although there was no noticeable limp in her step or frailty in her posture, a cane always came with her. It was no ordinary cane, but a merciless extension capable of igniting the strongest fears. Its jarring blows against the parquet, the barre or, on rare occasions, an unfortunate limb, reverberated throughout the whole of the Opera House.

"And grand-pliés!" she ordered halfway through as the bends became deeper, and the knocks of her cane gained momentum. Across the room, the napes of girls' necks perspired, and even breaths transformed into poorly concealed spasms. Despite varying age and experience, every pupil was subjected to the same warm-up. It was not long before the unison began to break down. The movements became less malleable, and the visual disorder resembled heads of wild wheat quavering every which way in a windy pasture. Dessa found the disharmony of bodies to be quite cheerful and contributed to the medley by deliberately skipping a beat. In an advanced rehearsal, this would merit immediate punishment, but the sheer size and diversity of the group left room for a bit of mischief.

A final knock of the cane allotted a moment of rest, and the girls shook out their limbs, preparing for the relevés that would surely follow. Asserted by the Mistress, Sasha started a fresh intermezzo, this time by Ponce. Tendus, retirés passés, ronds de jambes, frappés, and a set of sous sous concluded the warm-up. A liberal two-minute break was issued, and upon everyone's return, the lesson carried on with floor work to the upbeat tempo of Chopin's mazurkas. The girls made half a dozen lines with the shortest participants in front and braced themselves for a gruelling hour of pirouettes, jetés, and fouettés, with a special emphasis on pas de bourreé and its variations.

As the rehearsal ran its course and wound down to a finish, the pupils formed a line in front of the Mistress. One by one, they curtsied in gratitude, grabbed their belongings, and headed out. Some received a rare shoulder tap, the highest form of flattery and a heads up for exceptional work. Dessa frequently indulged in this gesture, but as her turn neared and she bent down into a low curtsy, the woman stood still.

"Too much fooling about," she said curtly without a second look.

"My apologies, Mistress," replied Dessa and hopped out into the corridor with her head hung low. She waited for Klara, who was held up at the very end of the line. A striking blonde came near, twirling a gold bangle with her index finger.

"Looks like the pet has left her Master's good graces."

"Hi, Inna."

"Where are we going this time?"

"Klara and I are heading home."

"You are not! And if you don't take me along, I am going to tattle."

Inna Dvorkina was the thirteen-year-old daughter of a shoe salesman who hit it big in illegal commerce smuggling Italian loafers into his otherwise modest footwear boutique. He started out as an ordinary cobbler, having recently rubbed elbows with several well-to-do folks on the bootleg market who promised him a speedy ascent into riches. Rumour was that Mister Dvorkin supplied the finest men's footwear to the theatre's artistic director and chief conductor in exchange for enrolling his princess in the city's finest dance academy.

For the most part, Dessa was quite indifferent to the girl. It was Inna who sought her out and leeched on, threatening to sabotage all adventure if she were to be excluded. Dessa could not fathom the persistence with which Inna schemed herself into their affairs. The blonde was less enthusiastic about Klara, but knew Dessa would never abandon her and said little aside from an occasional snide remark, which was met with instant hostility.

"Fine," Dessa said after a brief pause, "you are buying the tokens."

She looked right through the blonde to see if Klara was ready. The Mistress already made her exit, and the students dispersed. She peeked inside the studio and saw Sasha exchanging words with Klara near the baby grand. As he stroked her arm, she lowered her eyes, struggling to control a widening smile. Dessa understood he was up to no good.

"Let's go, Klara!" she interrupted and started down the hall without a moment's wait. The girl popped out of the room and hustled along, noticing their party had grown by one yet again.

The trio bid farewell to the Opera House and, after a crafty dance through a maze of alleyways, dove into the gusty vestibule of the Golden Gates metro station. Inna went straight to the cashier's booth to buy tokens.

"She threatened to rat us out again, not much I could do."

Klara nodded.

"What did he say to you back there?"

"Oh, that I danced very well today."

Familiar words used to lure another lamb, Dessa thought.

"He didn't mean it."

The frank response startled Klara, but she did not detect malice or jealousy in her friend's voice. Something was amiss, and Dessa refused to say another word about it.

Inna hurried over with a handful of tokens, and they proceeded to the escalators. The journey would be lengthy; this particular station was the deepest underground point in the city. Dessa relished every second of the way down. The smell of burned rubber saturated the tunnel and was one of her favourite aromas. Klara took her hand and held on tight. Inna was growing impatient.

"I demand to know where we are going. Father expects me home at two o'clock for a French lesson."

"You invited yourself," snapped Dessa and reached into her satchel. She took out a worn, pocket-sized leather address book and flipped through to a bent page. The trio stepped off the escalator and advanced to the platform hall.

"M... M.V. Located at 8/9 Bromski Boulevard. Apartment 37. No telephone number."

Klara scratched her head.

"I think that's at the end of the line on the Left Bank."

"Come on then, we can ask on the way."

Dessa closed the book and marched confidently to the front end of the eastbound platform. The girls followed her lead. Crossing the hall was a dramatic undertaking. Its length was extensive. Its domed ceiling featured a row of heavy bronze chandeliers adorned with candle-shaped bulbs. Its walls, held up by imposing broad columns of honed white marble, were covered in mosaics to evoke interiors of ancient orthodox cathedrals. Even the most unconcerned could not pass by without taking notice.

Like clockwork, the metro arrived every three minutes during the afternoon's peak hours. Judging by the drove of people, the train was due any second. Dessa stepped closer to the edge and glanced into the dark tunnel. A cool breeze came first, escalating into heavier gusts of air. Women's skirts fluttered; men's gazettes folded. A mounting rumble was followed by a dot of light that quickly grew.

The train came to a halt, its sliding doors opened and the girls were swept off their feet by a stampede of eager passengers. Klara and Dessa clenched hands, but Inna was pushed toward the back of the car and remained out of sight. The subsequent station was announced over the intercom, the doors shut and a friendly jolt propelled the trio on their next great adventure.

14

Chapter 3

The matter of the address book arose unexpectedly one evening on the way home from school. Dessa and Klara met at a nearby kiosk and agreed to explore the grounds of a newly erected embassy in the neighbourhood. A boy in Dessa's year claimed to have found a stash of rubles with a gold band in a tossed cigarette pack, and ever since, all of the children had gone mad searching for their own miniature treasures. Dessa figured he was full of it until she and Klara stumbled upon a ciggy pack of their own and discovered not only a couple of rubles, but a working lighter and leftover tobacco sticks. It seemed odd to place items of value in something so easily forgettable and disposable, yet the men made a bad habit of it, much to the delight of young scavengers, who quickly turned it into a sport.

Once the girls reached the embassy grounds and completed a preliminary loop, they passed by a row of mulberry trees, hoping to seek out a nice spot for extended observation. Because the building was brand new, its grounds were exceptionally clean and a disappointment to anyone in search of dropped or abandoned knick-knacks. They would have to settle for a dose of voyeurism instead.

The workday was rounding off and employees would be exiting the premises shortly. The girls hoped to see some dapper gents and stunning dames, for they imagined only the most attractive and polished need apply for a position at the highly regarded French Consulate. As they nestled under one of the lower hanging branches, Dessa espied a faded leather address book resting in a nearby flowerbed. She crawled over and snatched it up, swiftly returning to the comfortable shadows.

"We're in luck!" she exclaimed, showing off her find.

Klara flipped thoroughly through each page, and a unique pattern began to take shape. "An address book with no names?"

"Just initials, addresses—and some stand-alone numbers. It is rather odd."

"And what of these symbols?" continued Klara, pointing to a list of strange equations on the inside cover of the book.

"Perhaps a code of some sort."

"For what?"

"Beats me—"

"We should return it."

"There is no name inside, no forwarding address."

"It probably belongs to someone at the embassy."

"I doubt it."

Dessa was quite fixed on keeping their new acquisition. Klara was less certain.

"We really should take it in to make sure."

Dessa got up in a huff and started toward the lobby. She disappeared inside and did not come out for what seemed like a good fifteen minutes. Worried, Klara traced her friend's steps and prepared to enter the building when Dessa gleefully emerged.

"It's not theirs," she cheered. "We get to keep the spoils!"

Since then, their challenge was to visit a new address from the address book each week. Most locations turned out to be

16

ordinary residences with no explicit connection to each other. The girls never approached anyone and kept a safe distance. The real thrill was in taking trips to often-unknown corners of the city to satisfy their naturally sprouting curiosities.

It was by unfortunate chance that Inna got involved in the matter when, after a regular Friday rehearsal, she decided to follow them home. The first detour raised minimal suspicion and she thought nothing of it, though with each week it became increasingly clear that a secret project was in motion. Whatever it was, she could not stand to be left out, so the threats of exposure began. Unwilling to have their excursions cut short, Dessa complied.

&

Metro stations zoomed past one by one, and within a half hour the trio was on the Left Bank of the Dnepr River. A few brief inquiries yielded exact directions to their destination. When the train pulled up to the final platform, they darted through the doors and up the escalators, eager to step above ground.

The Left Bank, located on the east side of the river, was a predominantly residential area with a mix of factories and other industrial structures. The Right Bank housed the older portions of the city, its history, and vast cultural treasures. It was widely considered a haven for the upper classes and the intellectual elite, while people of simpler professions lived on the left side, breaching the gap daily for work. For Dessa, no part of the city was off limits.

As they walked farther away from the metro station, people and automobiles became scarce. There was a dreadful kind of silence in the air, an eerie, haunted feel of abandonment. Inna was getting nervous.

"This all looks very deserted," she said. "Maybe we should turn back."

"I've no intention of doing that," Dessa replied, unfazed.

17

Inna was as anxious to move forward together as she was to walk back alone, but continued on. They stopped abruptly at a crosswalk, and Klara pointed to a street sign on the right. Bromski Boulevard. The apartment building should have been somewhere along the street. They were close. Dessa took the lead and, in a matter of minutes, they were facing a drab five-story Khrushchyovka, 8/9. There were multiple entrances, none of which had any discernible codes.

"Plain walk-ins, five to a floor," mumbled Dessa and started toward the second entryway.

Indoors, the trio headed straight for the stairs. Before they could reach the third landing, a door opened above, and an older woman came into view. She passed them on the staircase without any acknowledgement, and for a split second, they felt an unnerving chill travel along their spines. A strong sense of distress infused the air, and Dessa noted a stack of pamphlets in the woman's pale, ghostly hands, a grainy photograph, and a list of coordinates. A "last seen on..." And then she was gone.

The girls kept on. Trying to shake off the odd feeling, they braked in front of the woman's doorway. It was apartment 37.

Chapter 4

On 25 August 1991, Dessa's eleventh birthday was considerably overshadowed by a shocking turn of political events. The night prior, in a tedious, day-long live broadcast, heads of state announced that an Act of Independence was signed, and the country had separated from the USSR. It was a glorious conclusion to a month of turbulence, chiefly the August Putsch, where hardline members of the Communist Party tried and failed to remove Gorbachev from power.

Telephones rang; tongues wagged. There was little else of greater importance to discuss.

Dessa worried that, in light of such circumstances, her birthday celebrations would be put on hold, but was assured all would go on as planned. Traditionally, two parties were held every year, one for the children, the other for older family and friends. Dessa was partial to the adult variety, where champagne flowed freely, the discourse was bolder, and the laughs more plentiful. Shurik would be at his finest, entertaining the crowd with a heavy dose of buffoonery whilst catering to every whim of his darling granddaughter.

As per usual, the children's party was scheduled first. This year, the guest list included Inna Dvorkina, along with some classmates from the Braga Lyceum. Klara was never invited.

The young guests, some accompanied by their mothers, arrived at half past one. Everyone was in high spirits, dressed to the nines. The boys looked sharp in suit trousers and starched shirts as they handed over a stunning bouquet of peach gladiolas. The ladies were equally primped in elegant taffeta gowns, their hair curled and held by silk ribbons.

Inna triumphantly presented a festively decorated package, and all watched eagerly as Dessa unwrapped the goods. The contents pleasantly surprised her, and with a wide grin, she took out a beautiful, blue-haired Malvina doll. Malvina was a popular character from Alexey Tolstoy's children's novel The Golden Key, or the Adventures of Buratino, a Soviet rendition of Collodi's Pinocchio fairy tale. The doll was a dream of every girl, a symbol of etiquette, nobility, and polished elegance.

Dessa sincerely thanked her guests and encouraged them to join her for an afternoon of games, prizes, and wild fun. Mother brought in a two-tier chiffon cake to complement an already crammed table of cocoa pastries, marzipan sweets, and a towering croque-en-bouche. Dessa blew out her candles in a single instance, and applause echoed throughout the room. The tea party was in full swing.

Soon after, the buzzer rang, and one of the mothers sprinted through the hallway to open the front door. A sheepish girl came into view.

"And you are?"

There was a faint indiscernible whisper.

"Lara? Oh, Klara." She turned back, shouting to Dessa's mother, "It's the Jewish girl, should she come in?"

"No, that isn't necessary. Tell her Dessa will come out for a minute."

The birthday girl listened in disbelief.

"Make it quick, and don't keep your guests waiting."

In no particular hurry, Dessa shuffled to the front door and peeked out onto the landing. Klara was waiting patiently with a square package accented by a white ribbon.

"Happy birthday," she said.

"Mm-hmm. Is that my present?"

Glimpsing the lush doll, the beautiful flowers, and the table of delicacies, Klara shied away.

"It's nothing so lovely."

"Are you going to let me have it or not?"

Klara handed over the gift and lowered her head as Dessa feverishly dug into the wrap. Her eyes froze.

"–Dostoyevsky?"

"I couldn't buy a proper gift, and there wasn't much else in the house. I'm sorry."

"Don't be foolish, this is a fantastic offering!"

Mother was calling on Dessa to re-join her guests.

"Wait right here," she said and swiftly retreated inside. Some minutes passed before she re-emerged with a makeshift box of dessert. All the delectable treats Klara spied in the distance were there and in abundance.

"For you. I wish you could partake in the festivities, you know Mother–"

"I understand."

"No, you don't. Better yet, you shouldn't. She is in the wrong. They all are."

Klara cracked a weak smile and turned on her heel toward the stairs. Dessa pulled her back in, playfully kissed her on the lips, and let go.

"Thanks for the book," she winked and shut the door.

Bemused, Klara brushed her fingertips across her mouth.

After everyone left, Dessa lounged in her bedroom surrounded by birthday gifts. Klara's white ribbon rested in her lap. The distinct feel and aged smell of the book she held enticed her. The words of Dostoyevsky's Crime and Punishment aroused great curiosity.

Chapter 5

Hours morphed into days, and days into weeks, as Kievans chipped away faithfully at their thinning, one-a-day kitchen calendars. September imposed an air of sobering routine, churning the masses, sedating them into October's comparably sombre disposition.

An uncommonly wet November rounded out the season. Temperatures dropped. Morale dipped. Twilight blanketed the cityscape for much of the waking hours as heavy thunderstorms pounded the skyline. Umbrellas contorted under pressure while even the sturdiest rain slickers and galoshes left their occupants drenched. Sums of water engulfed the streets, and wild gusts of wind rendered all human defenses powerless.

The majority of the people had leaks in their residences. Elevators buzzed with accounts of dripping ceilings, chipped walls, and flooded balconies. No one wanted to be outdone and exaggerated the damage with every subsequent retelling.

ن

Dessa's workload at the Braga Lyceum was becoming a real drag. It was not the difficulty of her assignments, but their sheer volume that left no time for personal affairs. Aside from the brief walks to and from the ballet academy, she had not spent any amount of time with Klara. Their weekly excursions were indefinitely put on hold. Days became shorter, curfews more stringent, the weather more dreary. Time was of the essence.

Shurik was on tour in Tbilisi, and Dessa was often granted permission to visit his neighbouring apartment on the condition she phoned to check in regularly and engaged exclusively in piano rehearsals, homework, or reading. An ideal time to sneak meetings with Klara, she thought, except her friend had a comparably active schedule, disallowing for extracurricular meetings.

Shurik's personal library was a haven for any bibliophile and housed full collections of both Russian and foreign literature. He frequently boasted that his assortment had a book for any occasion and took on the challenge to excite the curiosity of even the most uninterested reader. In spite of the rich selection, only one novel currently held Dessa's interest. It was the same novel that transfixed her months ago, and she was rereading it for the third time. There was a special corner for Dostoyevsky on one of the upper shelves. Strangely enough, all his works were present save for one. Crime and Punishment was nowhere to be found, and Dessa was ever thankful to have obtained Klara's copy. The knowledge gained with every reading proved it a gift that was anything but ordinary, for its ideas nourished the psyche and lingered long after the pages were turned. The text brimmed with nuances she was much too young to digest, and yet, there was a feeling of absolute necessity to understand. To solve the moral ambiguities, the sources of anguish and motivation, was to unlock the very mystery of the human condition.

She was there, immersed in the story, the quiet, and the darkness that was manifest in each page. Overcast skies with

24

violent winds tempted her to stay put in the massive, leather chair where she habitually dwelled. Bathing in the contrasting warmth of the library and Grandpapa's wool throw, Dessa slipped in and out of the realm of consciousness. Her arms grew heavy, the book heavier. To hold it any longer was an inconceivable challenge. As she let go, her body followed.

In a remote corner of her mind, a key was inserted then turned, deadbolts shifted, and a door opened. She waited for it to close. The auditory validation never came. There were odd thumps and laughter in the foyer, then the corridor, then the dining room. Drawers opened. Glasses clinked. Another key, another door, this time to the liquor cabinet. A cork popped, spirits poured, a toast was made. A female voice drew nearer to the library and stopped abruptly. The door creaked open, and Dessa was roused from her slumber.

"It's just my niece," a deep male voice sighed with relief.

The girl rubbed her eyes and looked up. A burly man of mid-thirties stood in the doorway. He was extravagantly dressed and well groomed, contrasting the condition of his Chesterfield overcoat, which stunk of whiskey. Upon closer inspection, his wrists revealed a set of abstract tattoos he kept hidden even in the sweltering heat of summer. When pressed by the girl, he claimed they were a mark of his army years, though she believed them to retain a more astute, sinister meaning.

"Uncle Leo!"

"Hello, my darling."

A voluptuous, red-lipped, raven-haired woman walked in.

"Who is she?"

"This is my friend, Natasha," he said and brought her closer.

She knelt in front of the club chair and extended her well-manicured hands toward the girl's face. The mink fur brushed against Dessa's collarbones as Natasha gave her cheeks a light squeeze. Natasha was dripping in gold, her clothing impeccably

25

tailored, and her scent rare and expensive. Everything about her was luxurious.

"What a doll!" she laughed.

Leo scanned the shelves, mumbling numbers under his breath. His gaze rested on a set of French art books.

"Which will fetch more, Nat, Renaissance or Baroque?"

"Hey, you can't take those!"

Natasha pinched the girl's shoulder to calm her down.

"Silly lassie, we aren't taking them for good, we just want to have a look."

"They aren't yours to take," she protested. "Grandpapa would never allow it."

"Grandpapa doesn't need to know," Leo said sternly, strolling over and perching himself up on the chair's armrest. "Are you really going to betray your dear uncle?"

"That is not fair."

"Isn't it?"

"Scolding me while you betray the trust of your own father. It's unjust."

He leaned into her and stroked his chin, carefully framing his thoughts.

"Would you like to hear a secret?"

She nodded.

"No act is unjust, darling, when your reasons are justified. You see, everything you want is yours for the taking. If you need it, and you have a good reason to need it, then you can take it. People will tell you that you can't, but you can. And you should."

He paused for a moment of reflection, and his face twisted into a self-gratifying grin.

"On second thought, I suppose it isn't much of a secret, but I am willing to bet no one has ever told it to you quite like this."

"As a matter of fact, your reasoning is fairly in tune with that of Raskolnikov."

26

He looked at her book and broke out in maniacal laughter. "Aren't you a tad young for this sort of literature?"

She wondered how big a fool they thought she was. "I won't let you take them."

Exasperated, the adults exchanged a knowing glance, and Leo finished off with an affirmative dip of the head.

"Alright, don't get worked up. We'll leave everything as is."

Dessa was distrustful of the sudden retreat.

"Come on then, let's go to my room. I've a pair of new soldiers to show you," he said.

"You mean it?" Dessa asked.

"Yes, my dear."

Leonid Faustov was an architecture school dropout whose real trade was sculpting. He claimed it was an unprosperous talent at its best and a vexing burden at its worst, as there was no niche for it in the current cultural climate, and verbal accolades proved insufficient without a monetary commitment. Staging weekly displays on Andreyevsky Descent in anticipation of haggling over meagre rubles was a novice pastime, and no one else was willing or able to rightfully compensate his genius.

His exact profession was now a mystery, although the drinking, gambling, and sporadic disappearances pointed to a life of recklessness and, in all possibility, elite crime. He had use of a lavish room at Shurik's apartment, and on the rare occasions he was there, took time to sculpt a miniature White Guard. The hobby thrived on account of his fascination with the Civil War and later the Great Purge, where much of the Faustov clan faced the firing squad. To complete the Guard was to avenge something in his innermost self. The project garnered unconditional, earnest effort, and Leo regarded himself as a revolutionary of sorts in undertaking it.

A true artist's abode, his room was home to the baby grand Ibach, stacks of sketching pads, and boxes of Plasticine. Half-

27

empty bottles of cognac and overflowing ashtrays were scattered about on the parquet. The air was thick.

Natasha moaned and turned to the window.

"The handle is broken, don't bother."

"Well, I can't stay here a moment longer."

"Then go to the dining hall."

She fussed with her fur, throwing it carelessly on Leo's bed, and took off her wristwatch.

"I'm going to wash these," she said, gathering the ashtrays and various glassware.

He waved her off and lifted a tarp on a corner coffee table, revealing a full-fledged Imperial Guard underneath. The cavalry and infantry were carved with awe-inspiring precision. A batch of roughed-out lancers and hussars rested in a separate crate. All were about five centimetres tall and solid grey, for no modelling paint was yet applied.

Leo took off his Chesterfield and dinner jacket. Rolling up the sleeves of his shirt, he held out his arms and flexed his fists. It was their game of makeshift monkey bars, and Dessa was all too happy to hang freely on his strong, muscular wrists. Having sufficiently entertained his niece, Leo brought her to the coffee table and lodged her in his lap. He took two miniatures from a far row and placed them on the edge of the stand.

"What do you think, my love?"

"Oh, they are exquisite, Uncle Leo!" she cheered, examining the figurines. "Save for they're different from the rest."

"You are quite right."

"This one, for example, is no soldier at all." She pointed at a long-robed mould.

"That's because this one is a priest."

"A priest! What's he got to do with the White Guard?"

"I'm afraid this endeavour is no longer about the Guard as it is about Russian Nobility."

28

"Will they still fight?"

"Yes, and all will lose."

"Even the priest?"

"Especially the priest."

"Do you know him?"

"I know of him."

"What is his name?"

"Father Konstantin, your thrice great-grandfather."

"What happened to him?"

"He was shot by the firing squad in '37."

"What for?"

"For being a righteous man, I presume."

"Did he die young?"

"Fifty-nine."

"Can we visit his grave?"

"There is no grave."

"Then where is he resting?"

"Nobody knows."

Their mounting silence was interrupted by intermittent sounds of clattering dishes in the kitchen. After a long pause, Dessa's eyes swelled with tears.

"How about that one?" she pointed at the other miniature.

"An officer, one of high distinction. Your great-great uncle."

"He has a nice sword."

"Not just any sword, an Imperial Golden Weapon, a gift from the Tsar himself for extraordinary gallantry."

"And he was shot, too?"

"Indeed."

"But, he was a brave soldier."

"All the more reason to die."

"I don't understand—"

"We are all that is left, my darling. They exterminated our dynasty like vermin."

29

"But why?"

He gently wiped her cheeks, kissing her forehead.

"Nobility, artistry, science, free thinking; it's all too dangerous, you see, too contagious and much too powerful. They wanted us to be like everyone else. We never were. The sole way to bring the intelligentsia down was to throw them in a mass grave to never be seen or heard from again."

"That's all changed now, isn't it, Uncle?"

"How do you mean?"

"Aren't we free at last?"

He chuckled at her naiveté.

"I expect we are, sport. I expect we are."

Natasha was back and eager to leave.

"Please, Leo. I am famished, and there isn't a morsel in sight."

"I'd rather you not rattle me this way, Nat. We have plenty of time."

"I've been more than patient with you, and now I'd like to go."

He threw her a cold stare and carried Dessa to the bed.

She watched him roll down and button his sleeves, pull on the jacket and then the overcoat.

"We appear to have some engagements. Promise to be a good girl, and I'll let you stay here as long as you lock the door on your way out."

"I'll be good."

"That's what I like to hear."

He led Natasha out, and the two disappeared in the hallway. Shortly, the front door opened and slammed shut. Dessa was alone once more.

She got up and trailed lazily to the library to retrieve her reading materials. The lights were still on, and Natasha's perfume lingered in the air. She folded the throw and picked up

30

her book, along with a stack of children's magazines. Checking the shelf with Parisian art collections, she was relieved to find the volumes in place. A shelf several metres to the left, however, exposed a glaring hole. Anxiously, she neared the spot. Among the many publications dedicated to Italy's High Renaissance, two exclusive tomes on Michelangelo and Raphael were missing.

Panic set in as she traced over the steps. Uncle Leo was with her at all times, contrary to Natasha, whose generous cleanup efforts left her to roam freely about the flat. The conniving snake must have hidden the books in her mink coat on the way out. Uncle was in on it, of course, yet Dessa's rage was directed entirely at his female accomplice.

She marched back to his room bent on destruction, but before she could reach the White Guard, she caught a sparkle out of the corner of her eye. In the crevice between Leo's bed and wardrobe lay a delicate woman's wristwatch. She inspected the find; an obscenely high-priced Cartier model that was likely bootlegged, for no store could legally carry such excess. The absence of something so expensive would soon to be noticed, and the tramp was bound to return in search of her lost treasure.

"Better to not wear anything you can't afford to lose, because you will never see it again," Dessa mouthed spitefully.

She dropped the watch in her sweater pocket, switched off the lights, locked the doors, and headed home.

ह•

The year ended in spectacular scandal. Shurik returned from Tbilisi, furious at the sight of his depleted collection. He argued with Leo, not about the financial damages, but the loss of priceless historical valuables and the readiness with which his own son partook in expediting a kind of cultural vacancy. The books were likely pawned to dealers who had no knowledge of their real worth beyond the heavy payout.

31

Leo countered that there was no reason to live in a vacuum of intellectual prestige, and that none of this accumulated bourgeois property held any significance outside of immediate monetary gains.

Dessa struggled to rationalize how Uncle Leo could have so much compassion for his 'exterminated' ancestors, yet so effortlessly forfeit any distinction indicative of them, their class, and their time.

In the midst of it all, Natasha was demanding her watch. When a thorough apartment search yielded nothing, she accused Dessa of theft, with an additional rummage of her belongings turning up empty.

"You sold it, didn't you?" she seethed.

"I've no need for that kind of money, and who would buy anything so expensive from a kid, anyhow?"

"Then you are hiding it!"

Dessa did not see how the disappearance of the watch was so different from the loss of the books, aside from the fact that one was replaceable and the other was not.

In truth, she hadn't a clue of the item's current whereabouts. On her way home that fateful evening, she dropped the watch into a storm drain as carelessly as Uncle Leo and his vamp chose to surrender a lifetime treasure for a seat at the poker table.

Chapter 6

A December referendum confirmed the inevitable, and by the end of the month, the Soviet Union officially ceased to exist. For the first time in the span of their existence, people celebrated the New Year as citizens of a sovereign nation.

1992 brought with it a torrent of innumerable change. The key concept of this newfound freedom was "opportunity": the opportunity to own property; the opportunity, without tedious wait-lists and paperwork, to buy a foreign-made car; the opportunity to travel beyond the Iron Curtain on a tourist visa; the opportunity to start a private business; and, most importantly, the opportunity to leave.

Grocery shops, clothing markets, and appliance emporiums underwent a magnificent transformation from thorough emptiness to an overstock of foreign goods. With the arrival of competition and a sweep of Soviet products out of sight, a consumerist haven was taking shape.

There was much gossip in the Faustov household about a certain middle-aged neighbour, Vasily, who spruced up his modest income as a bookkeeper by travelling monthly to Poland

and Hungary to buy up suitcases worth of cheap clothing his wife later marked up and sold at local rag fairs. Another fellow, upon privatizing his residence, decided to drill into the common attic and install a monstrosity of a Jacuzzi that he claimed transformed his otherwise average apartment into a Western abode of luxury. "This is how the Americans live!" he boasted to everyone in the elevators. All over, people were delirious with 'opportunity.'

≥▲

Dessa's winter months passed without incident. In a time of change, her life took on a monotonous routine. Mother was consistently inconsistent. She stopped making breakfast and gave Dessa supper leftovers that were either unevenly heated or served entirely cold. The girl wondered if this was an absentminded quirk, a byproduct of the busyness that came with 'opportunity,' or if, perhaps, a more menacing undertone was at play.

Whatever meals were made tasted so awful, even the strays in the courtyard balked at their sight. The flat was an utter mess, and while the girl completed what chores she could, there was a general atmosphere of disregard and disarray. Day by day, the apartment shifted from one of mother and child to that of an unattached, prowling female. The woman spent most of her mornings in front of the mirror and much of her evenings on the telephone discussing men Dessa knew nothing about.

During work hours, she was a secretary to a twice-divorced, middle-aged man, who owned a chain of confectionaries around the city. The job was below her pay grade and social status, but she held on, hoping to rope the rich sucker in, or at the very least, meet another through his vast network of contacts. Finding a man was difficult enough; keeping one after the big reveal of single motherhood was next to impossible. Dessa sensed deep resentment, a burgeoning malice in Mother's sour

34

demeanour for being a perpetual roadblock in the ever-delicate matters of companionship.

The question of the absent father was rarely raised, his departure shrouded in total mystery. From what she understood, a divorce took place hardly two years after her birth, one that resulted in a sign-over of all parental rights. There were rumours that the family made her father a monetary offer he could not refuse on the condition to never show his face in their parts. Wedding slides and all legal documentation were conveniently missing. Close friends of the family regularly teased her as a child of the moon, for there was no trace of him in her character or appearance. There were days where she reckoned it might very well be true, yet her patronymic stated otherwise. As Dessa Aleksandrovna Faustova, she deduced he was Aleksandr, and not a pinch more than that.

The girl was plagued by sentiments of escape and tried her best to find refuge at the Braga Lyceum, the dance academy, or even at Lady Rama's, a vain quest of hopping amid hostile environments.

The Lyceum transformed into yet another establishment of "opportunity" where extravagant bouquets, sweets, perfumes, and scarves became the desired currency for securing high marks. Those, whose parents could not afford such expenses, were cast aside, and no amount of academic excellence would sustain them at the top of their class without a hearty donation.

Meanwhile, at the Opera House, pupils endured increasing cruelty from Mistress Galina, who acquired a new accessory in the form of a knout that caught someone unawares just about every rehearsal. The appetite for success was so overwhelming that rarely did anyone dare speak up, and the few who did were shunned by their families and told to work harder.

Most peculiar, however, were the piano lessons at Lady Rama's where Dessa continued to track a pattern of unfamiliar, out-of-place items. The strange moccasins in the summer were followed by a gentleman's umbrella, a wool scarf, a smoking pipe and, quite recently, a pair of leather gloves. While a suitor appeared to be frequenting the premises, it was unlikely the articles belonged to a singular person. The umbrella was too expensive, the pipe too cheap, the scarf provincial, and the gloves were those of a workingman. Because it was a severe clash of style and financial resources, Dessa favoured a theory of multiple guests, albeit the purpose of these visits was a mystery. Rama did not possess the body, face, or age of a desirable mistress. What possible interest she held for them remained unclear and merited advanced investigation.

❧

In February, Dessa and Klara briefly resumed excursions under the pretext of going to ride on their toboggans. They made three more visits to similar residences, all on the Left Bank, with no extraordinary breakthroughs. Dessa was growing frustrated at the lack of connectivity between the addresses. The address book was clearly written in code, not meant for casual eyes and, therefore, had to come together in a thrilling reveal. On the other hand, there were merely two addresses left, one of which seemed non-existent. Either someone took great care to masquerade the real location or, in a more probable and banal twist, simply made a mistake.

The silver lining to these uneventful trips was Inna's rising absence. Because the girls started the journeys from home and not the Opera House, Inna was cast out of their affairs without difficulty. Furthermore, she was less sociable than usual and seemed genuinely uninterested in tagging along. Dessa figured her aloofness was caused by Inna's daddy's business troubles, for in the midst of post-Soviet 'availability,' his fine Italian goods were no longer exclusive or even desirable. Word spread quickly, and there were rumours Inna may lose her spot at the academy unless her father could find another bargaining chip to seduce the faculty.

≥●·

It was now spring, with the school year rapidly coming to an end, and final exams were around the corner. Having estimated them to be a breeze, Dessa was not overly perturbed. An ambitious promotional undertaking at the ballet academy piqued her interest instead. In the final months of every dance season, a charming school performance was staged for the general public, showcasing the young talent from Mistress Galina's ensemble. By and large, the annual display was meant to satisfy families of the pupils, particularly those who would otherwise be excluded from the premier productions throughout the year. Nonetheless, many held high hopes of possible discovery and impending stardom, believing a sizable lot of scouts from popular dance troupes would surely be in attendance.

Basic brochures were distributed weeks in advance, but this time around, would be complemented by pocket calendars printed on thick paper stock with dimensions approximate of a standard playing card. Patrons could choose between three variations, and because the opening was scheduled for late May, the following summer months appeared most fitting. Each month's cover photo would feature a different set of dancers from the production, which was an anticipated debut by an aspiring local choreographer, Foma Djukin.

Damsels of Laylavie Springs was publicized as a spectacle of mass coordination that bypassed solo performances in favour of wowing the crowd with its command of synchronized dance. Djukin was a loyal proponent of beauty in numbers, not only welcoming, but demanding more bodies, more music, more stage sets, and costume changes. His vision centered on the adventures of three angelic sisters, who lived in the faraway, enchanted forest of Laylavie. The ninety-minute production was split into two acts and reflected the sisters' interactions with the forest's other inhabitants, including fairies, flowers, animals, and a group of wicked goblins. The admittedly primitive tale was more dazzling in its actual choreography and design, culminating in a grandiose march of close to 200 people. It would highlight a number of beloved folk dances, most notably a colourful rendition of the Hopak by the theatre's male ensemble, the Bereznianka, and the Trans Carpathian Dubotanets.

The sheer size of the project guaranteed a level of involvement for all. The pressing question now was casting the leads, even if the majority of their numbers would be performed in the presence of the corps de ballet. No official auditions were held, but to keep up appearances, Mistress Galina ordered an open rehearsal attended by Djukin himself. He drifted around the hall, cocking his head, stroking his chin, whispering to the Mistress, doing his best impression of a pensive choreographer.

A young, undoubtedly talented man of early thirties, he was more preoccupied with pandering to the image of an eccentric craftsman than the craft itself. The production would be a success, but it was the provocative gestures, the posing, and a heavy air of pretentiousness that Dessa found unflattering. She knew his presence was for show. The leads were chosen long ago behind closed doors. She did not care for the part one way or another, though her talent alone should have inspired the faculty to give her consideration. There were few others like her, and many relied on the names, wallets, and connections of their families to prosper.

After class, the pupils were given time to cool down while Djukin and the mistress presumably chose the finalists. Following a lengthy deliberation, he clapped his hands and called everyone to surround him in a large circle. He paced about with his hands resting comfortably on the hips. The clicks of his heels were calculated and underlined the stark certainty of his decision.

"Dvorkina," he said after a drawn out pause. The studio resonated with hushed gasps. A blatant fix, Dessa fumed, wondering what Mister Dvorkin could have possibly bribed the theatre heads with this time. An adequate technical dancer, Inna was by no means an expressive one, her range of motion dull, limited, and uninspired for a girl of such otherworldly beauty.

"Faustova."

Djukin motioned her to come up front. The gossip continued, this time with an undertone of envy, not mockery. The pick was logical and, in all probability, the least tainted by backdoor shenanigans.

"Feldblum will round out the lead trio, the rest will be divided into supporting troupes," he concluded and bowed out.

Dessa's heart sank. This was turning into a circus and she wanted no part of it. Her dearest Klara was hardly experienced to join the ranks of the advanced, much less take on a leading role. Something foul was afoot, and Dessa was determined to expose whoever put in the extra word, not to embarrass her friend, but for the simple knowledge and her own peace of mind. The Bibliotheca hours Yakov leveraged to secure his sister a spot at the barre would not hold any weight to get her into an actual show. Someone else had taken initiative.

On the way home, the girls walked in uncomfortable silence. Klara was mum on her newfound celebrity, knowing full well how odd it should have sounded to Dessa, who was now equally reserved, deciding to work out the mystery on her own.

In the elevator, eye contact was made at last when Klara prepared to exit on the third floor.

"You should be ready by ten so we can meet up with Inna at the station," Dessa grumbled.

"Alright, I'll meet you downstairs. Have a good night."

Klara jumped out and looked on as Dessa hastily pinned a call button, and the doors slid shut.

A break would have been swell at a time like this, but the girls, scheduled to meet for the calendar shoot at a remote portrait studio, had to endure each other's company as soon as the next morning. Although there were well-to-do photographers in the area, most were not readily available, or those who were, grossly overcharged for their services. Out of convenience, the supporting dance troupes would have their photo sessions at the theatre down the road, whereas the trio was told to pick up their costumes in the morning and head straight to the assigned studio, located close to shore on the Left Bank.

ᒑ

The next day, Dessa and Klara met promptly in the lobby at ten o'clock. The walk to the Opera House was wordless, no longer on account of earlier awkwardness. The two were lost in their own reflections, and the quiet suited them nicely.

At the theatre's costumier wing, a seamstress directed the girls to the proper chamber where, to Dessa's surprise, Inna already waited.

"Weren't we to meet at the station?" Dessa asked.

"I changed my mind. Besides, this way I'll make sure to get the right costume."

"What does it matter? They are all the same."

An assistant came from the storage room carrying three opaque garment bags. Each was tagged, and Inna rushed over to receive hers at once.

"May I take a look?"

"I'd rather you not fuss with it at this time, doll," said the assistant.

The other two were handed their bags, and Dessa started toward the exit.

"Come on. We can't be late, you can marvel at it there."

The trio slipped out of the theatre and bolted for the metro station. There was not a second to waste, so Dessa generously handed out her spare tokens, and the girls sprinted down the escalators. Minutes later, they boarded a train and were on their way, being careful not to crush their garment bags.

ই৯

For a business with the high-flown title of Regal Portraiture, there was hardly anything regal about it. The studio, hidden in a narrow side street, was housed in the tiniest of rental spaces, its entrance and unassuming sign so minuscule, the girls circled the area twice before finally stumbling upon it. No actual photographs graced the shop window, making the girls even more suspicious. After some reflection, they concluded the theatre could not possibly send them into an illicit environment, and proceeded inside.

The shopkeeper's bell chimed and a weathered, elderly man peeked out from the back room. He shuffled over, examining the trio from head to toe, and after a series of grunts, lit up with a shining smile of recognition.

"Ah yes," he said, rubbing his palms in delight, "the damsels!"

Inna remained standoffish.

"Pardon?"

"You are the Damsels of Laylavie Springs, are you not?" he continued playfully.

"Indeed, we are, sir!" responded Dessa with a curtsy.

"Don't tell me you've come all this way alone?"

"Indeed, we did."

He had a pleasant, almost magical demeanour, and she could not help but feel at ease in his presence.

"If you don't mind me saying, you look like Papa Carlo."

"Then by all means, refer to me as such if you so please," he laughed. "It so happens there was another lifetime, before any of you graced this earth, when I worked as a puppeteer's apprentice."

"You don't say!"

"It's the absolute truth. After the shoot, we can dust off the trunk and glance at the retired marionettes I made for the Puppet Theatre."

"That sounds splendid," she said, scanning the cluttered lobby. "Where should we change?"

"Oh, of course," he fussed, gesturing them to a curtained entryway. "Right through here, ladies."

What conveyed the impression of an abandoned, crumbling shanty on the outside, was turned into a breathtaking, spacious warehouse of mystical goods. It was divided into sections with various set pieces, each within its own time period and theme. Fabrics were draped over the furniture; props cluttered every nook and cranny; rolled-up rugs leaned in the corners. Lighting fixtures, tripods, and cameras rested in the centre. It was a place to make magic, a genuine workshop of storytelling.

He pointed to an exquisite French dressing screen. The trio receded out of view as he fiddled with the flash on his camera.

Behind the screen, another drama unfolded. When the girls unzipped the garment bags and took out their costumes, they were not, as Dessa originally made out, created equal. The powder puff tutus were only identical in style, not in their colour or embroidery, creating a visually discernable hierarchy of the soloists. While Inna and Klara's dresses were a solid white, Dessa's champagne-coloured tutu shimmered with delicate gold and silver threading, its bodice offset with strings of gemstones.

Inna was livid. "There must be some mistake," she huffed, trying the dress on for size. "All the same, hmm?"

"I honestly didn't know," said Dessa, but Inna had no interest in her explanations and tossed back the costume.

"Papa is not going to like it one bit," she continued, this time to herself, squirming into her own dress.

The rest of the way, they prepared in silence, pulling on their pointes and fixing their chignons. Dessa smudged some rouge

42

on her cheeks and passed it on to Klara, who did the same. Inna went a step further and lined her eyes, later dabbing a bit of colour on her lips.

As they emerged from behind the folding screen, the old man threw his hands up in exclamation. "What an angelic trio! Magnificent."

Dessa came forth and studied his camera, a GDR-made, 35mm Praktica. "Grandpapa has one exactly like it at home," she said, gently contouring the lens with her index finger.

"It's a wonderful camera," he replied, dusting off his light meter.

He directed the girls to a beautiful beige chaise longue, centering Dessa in the middle and the others by her side. On the first try, they sat facing the camera, their feet crossed, toes flexed and pointed at the ground. Later, they stood, holding their hands close to their hearts, feet in third position. The final photographs had them assembled with feet tucked under, backs turned, necks elongated, and faces in profile. Their eyes fixated on the camera, with only one daring to look straight through it.

As the session wrapped up, and the girls changed into their regular clothing, the old man shared with them his long-forgotten talent of puppet making. His trunk was full of defunct marionettes. Most had lost their strings, costumes were faded or torn, but the detail with which he had carved them was still remarkable. The blue-haired Malvina and her pal Buratino were found unexpectedly at the bottom of the trunk. He claimed they were the very first marionettes to be made in the likeness of Tolstoy's heroes.

The new find, this "Papa Carlo" and his enchanting quarters so expertly hidden from the naked eye, inexplicably excited Dessa. The man had lived an arresting life and had stories to tell with no one to listen. She wanted to change that and vowed to return as soon as her schedule allowed it.

It was now late afternoon, and the girls had to return their costumes before the seamstresses locked up. To gain a couple of minutes, they cut through a desolate courtyard in hopes of reaching the metro station faster. Passing by a horde of strays and a number of unconscious drunks, Dessa registered a message board out of the corner of her eye. Something on it looked vaguely familiar.

"Wait!" she shouted and slowed her pace to take a closer look. Under the glass panel hung a yellowing pamphlet of a missing woman. Dessa froze in her steps. The young woman. It was the same pamphlet she saw in the ghostly white hands so long ago. This had to be the daughter of the skeletal creature they encountered on the staircase last summer.

Another poster got her attention, this time on account of the address. She had seen it before. She had been there.

"It couldn't be—"

She dropped her garment bag and frantically ransacked her purse.

"What is it?" inquired Klara as they backtracked.

Inna was furious.

"If you make us late—"

"Quiet!" Dessa directed their attention to the board. "Just look." They complied as she turned page after page in the address book. "These addresses match, and here is another." She pointed to a third poster, its photo faded and address barely legible. "All missing."

"Very perplexing, what does it mean?" asked Klara.

"It doesn't have to mean anything," Inna argued. "That's three addresses out of how many?"

"There may be more," Dessa said, "all on the Left Bank, in these types of areas. Something perverse could be in motion." Inna shook her head and started down the footpath. Klara hesitantly followed.

"There must be more," Dessa reasoned with herself, taking up her garment bag and dashing toward the metro.

Chapter 7

The staircase between the fourth and fifth floors of Dessa's apartment complex was effectively falling apart. The stairs themselves, wrapping around a see-through elevator shaft, had deep cracks down the middle, their edges chipped and crumbling with every successive step. The metal handrails were rusty and porous to the touch, unlike the smooth and polished wood railings at lower levels. The original design accommodated four floors. In the early fifties, after the war, a fifth floor was added to maximize capacity and profit. As a result, much of its construction did not match the rest of the interior and looked thrown together on a whim, compared to the elegant architecture found elsewhere in the building.

Klara leaned against a freshly painted wall near the garbage chute. The coats of paint were lathered so thick that, even dry, it was gummy and left an unpleasant film upon contact with bare skin. Dessa was feeling behind a lofty pipe for a smokes pack. The chute had its own enclosure and was kept clean by the residents, making it a choice spot for puckish activity. The area was not readily seen from either landing, and the thin acoustics quickly alerted of a foreign presence, giving the girls ample time to disappear. She managed to get a hold of it and reached in for a cigarette. Klara lit a match. Dessa took a drag, blocked Klara with her arms, leaned in and kissed her, trying to transfer the smoke, only to break away in visible disappointment.

"You're not getting it right," Dessa scoffed.

"I don't like it."

"Because you can't do it well."

"I think it's wrong."

Dessa was unusually annoyed. "It's a silly cigarette."

"I meant the kiss."

"The 'kiss'?"

"Yes, like the one on your birthday." Klara was shamefaced, ready to hear the brunt of it. To her great surprise, Dessa had little to say.

"If you want to be a kid about it, then go play with your dolls. I am off."

"W–wait, where are you going?"

"I have a rendezvous with Sasha."

"A rendezvous?"

"Yes, you know, the kind you and he have after class sometimes," Dessa sneered. "Ciao!"

She descended the staircase, vanishing in the darkness, her footsteps echoing as Klara looked on.

The courtyard was a private space where some tenants occasionally parked their cars. It had a wide road that ran alongside the massive complex, accentuated by groomed flowerbeds and green zones with fruit trees, birches, weeping willows, and Lombardy poplar. It contained two playgrounds, one on each end, as well as a series of maintenance sheds for the gardeners, plumbers, electricians, and porters. The sheds, abundantly concealed by the weeping willows, could not be seen from residents' balconies and were rarely of any interest to anyone other than their intended personnel.

This particular evening, on the first Sunday of May, the courtyard was completely deserted, save for a pack of strays circling the area. It was the start of the May Day holidays, and nearly all able-bodied tenants were indulging at their dachas. Most would be gone all week. The Faustov clan also had a worthy retreat outside of Kiev, located in the small town of Boyarka, where Mother and her friends currently stayed. Dessa was granted reprieve to come along, proclaiming last minute that the Feldblums extended an invitation to their dacha instead; and Mother, in spite of her general disapproval, agreed at once.

"Thank goodness they took that brat off my hands," she later quipped. In reality, there was no invitation or even a dacha, but the truth held little importance, as Mother would not dare trouble herself to check on the mundane details.

⁊ఽ

Dessa soaked up and revelled in the freedom to roam about for days on end, her sole care to not be seen or heard by familiar faces. To reach the apartment building's yard using the structure's official exits required one to trek in a roundabout way, confronting leftover concierges and guards from the Finnish Consulate across the road. Fearing recognition, she chose to forego the common route and slipped in through a cluster of basement tunnels on the opposite side of the complex. The path less travelled landed her smack-dab in the middle of the courtyard without setting foot on the main road.

Heading straight for the sheds, she spotted a figure lurking in the distance. Sasha was already there.

"You're always late," he snarled.

"Relax, there's no one around to spy the smut you like."

He smacked his lips, pacing skittishly with hands in his pockets.

"Did you bring it?" she asked.

"It's not free."

"Let me see it first."

He fumbled in his pockets and took out a fine porcelain figurine. She extended her palm. He drew back.

"You get it after."

She knew there was no use arguing.

"Fine, you want to see?"

"No, I've seen plenty."

"Touch?"

"No."

"What then?"

"I want to feel inside."

She contemplated a moment, then flattened herself against the shed and, with an air of distain, reached under her skirt. After a few pulls, the white undies slid down her legs.

"Well?"

He was hesitant.

"Idiot. Think I'm going to stand like this all day?"

He came closer and ran his hand between her thighs.

She was unresponsive.

After mere seconds of amateur prodding, his face twisted into a frown. "You're getting hair already?"

"All women have hair there, and I am becoming a woman."

The pride with which the words came out repulsed him.

"If it was a woman I wanted, I wouldn't be wasting my time here with you, now would I?"

"You're more pathetic than I thought. Twenty-something twerp spending his free time diddling kids. You disgust me."

She jerked his hand free, pushed him away, and pulled up her garments.

He backed off, tensely licking the corners of his mouth. "You know what, Dessa? I think today is the day these pleasant sessions of ours are going to end. Sad to say, you no longer get the job done."

"You're a prick."

"Maybe so. Lucky for me, there's already someone to take your place, and one thing is for certain, she doesn't give any lip."

"Give me my figurine."

"No deal."

"Give it to me, or I'll tell everyone what a paedophile you really are."

He charged at her, clenching her throat, his hands shaking, saliva foaming.

"Listen, pint-sized wench, you're way out of your league."

"No, you are out of yours," she gasped, contorting her body to loosen his grip. "One word about what we've been doing here for the past year, and they will put you away for good."

He knelt to the ground, bringing the girl down with him.

"One peep, Dessa, one peep. And Klara is as good as dead. You hear?"

She fixed on him for what seemed like an eternity before a wave of cognizance swept over her face.

"It was you," she said with sharp assurance.

He threw her a quizzical look.

"You set her up for the part. Why? In return for what? What did she do for you? What did you make her do? Tell me!"

Sasha let go of her trembling body at last, striving to hide a broadening smirk. "And there we have it, the trump card." He wagged his finger. "I was sure it was jealousy when you kept spotting us together, and the upcoming ballet – well – you rarely like to share the spotlight, much less with anyone who is clearly undeserving. I see now, there's more to it. You actually care about her; in all your egoism you genuinely give a damn. Brilliant."

He patted her cheeks with the sweaty palms of his hands.

"This is precisely how I know, baby doll, everything will stay as is. You'll keep your mouth shut."

"I want my figurine," she sobbed.

"I already told you, no deal."

What transpired next would be recalled in great detail for months to come, granted, at that precise moment, there was no discernable continuity. It was now or never, anything pre-planned could fail as they were already on the outs, and chances were slim he would agree to meet again. Sasha may have been older, but gaunt. His grip was tight purely because he concentrated all of his might on the task. If she were to catch him unawares, he would fold. Odd instruments presented themselves to her – a rake, a mattock, a billhook, a scythe, a hoe, a shovel, all scattered about. It must have been the gardener's shed, she thought. Her mind drifted to Raskolnikov, to the coincidences that called on him to act and were now calling on her. It was explicit. This was her only opportunity.

Sasha was alarmed by the girl's atypical reserve. The sobbing stopped. She no longer trembled, her head was tilted, legs crooked, and arms long like a broken marionette. The abrupt emptiness after a colourful fit of temper made him oddly uncomfortable. For a split second, a gnawing feeling, somewhere deep in the underbelly, told him to get out now, or not at all. And yet, he waited, pitying her. He reached in his pocket and fished out the figurine.

"It's all yours, choke on it for all I care," he said, flinging it like a handful of kopecks at a lowly beggar. The figurine hit her temple, bounced in her lap, and rolled out of view. She was stock-still.

"Jesus Christ, you're a cretin," he moaned and shot her a final glance. Her appearance changed, a blink, a flash of sorts in the eyes. He turned on his heel, not understanding thereupon what it meant. It was rage.

The shovel may have been too heavy, the scythe out of reach, and the mattock's handle too short, for he was walking away, and she would have to get close. The nearest instrument was the garden hoe, and her arm, as if by its own will, grasped for it.

She came to her feet, took a step, then another and, with a soaring leap, swung the hoe at his head.

She expected him to topple over without incident much like the old pawnbroker and her half-sister. Unfortunately, this dull instrument was no axe, and she did not have the advantage of Raskolnikov's immaculate planning or even his aim.

Sasha staggered instead, twisting around in slow motion. Gaping at her in dismay, he poked at his left ear, extending his bloodied fingers in her direction.

She had to act fast for fear of his escape, but he had no intention of leaving. As she backed into a corner, feeling for the scythe, he barrelled at her with an inhuman shriek. His face was met with a sharp blade and warped into a grimace.

A swift, diagonal slash had cut his right eye, a part of his nose, and much of his mouth. Blood cascaded in rapidly swelling streaks. He was now partially blind and could not speak. Another slash followed, this time lower and with skilled precision, straight to the throat. He gasped for air as blood frothed at the wound, applying pressure with his hands. All efforts were in vain, and he eventually collapsed at her feet. When the blood began to pool, she casually stepped aside.

Fifteen minutes ought to have passed before Dessa registered the lifeless body and the intensity with which she continued holding the scythe. Sliding to the ground, she carefully set it down. Any similarities she imagined with Raskolnikov's crime should have ended right then and there. To leave the body as is would invite capture and prosecution. Was prosecution even essential? Or could an interrogation bring to light the filth of Sasha's character? He did it with her, with Klara and, in all likelihood, many others.

52

This was, without question, self-defence. Or was it? An investigator could potentially deduce that Sasha was hit from behind first and then slashed, posing no immediate threat. While his behaviour was undeniably appalling and worthy of punishment, was it worthy of death at her hands? In the current stream of political and cultural change, a sympathetic detective may very well be inclined to show lenience and gloss over the inconsistencies. On the other hand, he may not.

She wondered what was so undesirable about going to the station and reporting a paedophile, or why Sasha believed he had any leverage over her and could, therefore, keep on with his indecency. Even if she did engage in it willingly for quite some time, there was no reason to allude to her cooperation. Moreover, he could have blackmailed her to keep her mouth shut, threatened the reputation of her family and the families of others involved. In such a vicious cycle, all were made to comply. In order for the theory to work, however, everyone's stories had to be in accordance, and she had no idea if anyone, even Klara, was willing to turn this into a public spectacle. In other words, this violent climax was, without a shadow of a doubt, the most pragmatic solution to the problem.

Having reasoned the legitimacy of the crime, Dessa had to take action, to figure how to get rid of the body and where. Hiding it would ensure eventual discovery, no matter the state of its decomposition. It had to disappear without a trace.

The nunnery at the Saint Sophia Cathedral, located on the other side of the brick wall enclosing the courtyard, was getting renovated, with its residents temporarily displaced. Dessa lounged frequently on her balcony, watching over the masons, smelters, and carpenters at work. Lately, the crew laboured over flooring, retiling long-running porticos and sets of steps by the entryways, but, at present, they, too, were on holiday. With bountiful dirt, cement and tools at her disposal, she momentarily thought it a plausible scheme to bury the body there. She could drag him through the wicket gate and start digging. Yet, it soon occurred to her that what she observed from her balcony, the dwellers on the upper floors could very well observe from theirs.

Despite the slim possibility of anyone appearing right then, this was a task best left for after dark. For the time being, she would conceal his body in thick shrub along the wall.

With a deep inhale, she propped herself upright and took hold of his ankles. For someone so skeletal, he was heavy, causing her to wonder if the burial was, perhaps, an overly ambitious undertaking. With great strain, she pulled him to hiding and moved to take care of the blood that had already seeped into the sand. This part of the courtyard was not cobblestoned like the rest. A bit of sifting and sweeping around was enough for the evidence to wane.

She checked her clothes for spatter. Miraculously, it was minimal and barely showed on her already flecked, brightly coloured getup. She would scrub the hoe and scythe upon her return.

She picked up and dusted off the figurine, listening closely for the slightest rustle. Satisfied with the tranquillity of her surroundings, she moved away from the sheds, keeping in line with the shadows and, tiptoeing across the road, popped back into the basement of her apartment complex.

Dusk was on the horizon, and what minimal light happened to enter the underground was rapidly diminishing. Dessa felt her way down the narrow corridor, doing her best to remain unshaken by the echoing squeaks from the maintenance rooms along the way. The stench emanating from the chutes was unbearable. Garbage trolleys were on the brink of overflow and would not be rolled out for pickup until after Victory Day.

She emerged from the lower level and trod lightly up the stairs, consciously avoiding the explicitness of the old, rickety

54

elevator, for it could be heard at any time, by anyone, in the farthest parts of the building.

Between the second and third landings, she registered movement along the elevator shaft. Pausing, she turned her head and hastily stifled a shrill cry with her palms. A rat, of seemingly Herculean proportions, was climbing slowly up the wire netting of the shaft. Its body was at least a foot long, its tail even longer.

For a prominent residence, the building was experiencing a dire rat infestation, and the city had yet to do anything about it. Just last month, a neighbour's aging dachshund was gnawed to death in the furnace room after having wandered off during a routine midnight walk. The owner, living on the first floor, lowered the dog in a woven basket to roam about the courtyard. That night it did not return, and a search party of children was sent out the next morning to no avail until the waste collector, noting a peculiarly large rat gathering when passing through the basement, discovered a grisly scene of remains.

Since then, Dessa was even more fearful of the creatures, likening the largest, most revolting ones to the evil Mouse King from The Nutcracker. The creature was out of reach, but she scrambled past with great speed and, having arrived at the front door of her flat, retreated inside.

Calming her breath, she propped herself up against the coat rack. She was in total darkness and, to avert exposure, could not risk turning on any lights. In her delusions, she pictured the rodent nearing the landing, crawling closer and closer to the door, and waiting. Its comrades would soon rise from the basement, making the same tedious journey up the shaft; dozens upon dozens of Herculean rats clasping their paws at the chain links, surrounding the flat, taunting their prey.

Stumbling in the foyer, she got hold of a barely working flashlight from the shoe closet and progressed to her bedroom.

Once there, she dropped to her knees and pulled out a wooden jewellery box from under the bed. Inside, underneath sheets of tissue paper and scraps of velvet, lay a porcelain collection of animal figurines about a pinkie's length tall and fourteen in count. She held the new one tightly in her hand.

The acquisitions began over a year and some months ago, when she spotted the full collection, titled An Adventurer's Safari, in a shop window on a rainy afternoon. Instantly smitten, she begged and pleaded for even a single figurine, and because the price tag reflected its quality and exceptional craftsmanship, Mother would have none of it, branding Dessa an unruly child undeserving of something so precious. Yet, the girl's heart was set on it, and as if by fate, she soon discovered that the lanky pianist from her dance classes was employed as a casual clerk at that very place. When she inquired about the collection, their meetings began.

He was kind at first, unhesitatingly presenting her with a darling giraffe. They met privately every other week since, and with every consecutive tryst, the young man became bolder in his demands. On the whole, he preferred to have her deliver the sexual satisfaction, and it was only recently that he took the plunge, reversed their arrangement, and put his hands on her instead. He was clumsy and unsure of his fantasies; taking initiative had implications that were not present when he was merely a passive recipient of her services. Furthermore, her animal safari was nearly complete, and it was unclear what else, if anything, would entice her to continue their meetings. She was much too precocious to begin with, making the appeal of her youth stay solely in the physical body and not her mind. This was, precisely, why he started courting Klara. Two more figurines and he would be rid of Dessa for good.

Today's model was of a sable antelope. A single piece was left to collect, the opulent savannah elephant.

56

Dessa stirred from her sleep, realizing she had dozed off. Her bedroom was illuminated, yet the flashlight had long gone out. The source was the Sophia Cathedral, lighting up nightly around nine o'clock. Her eyelids grew heavy, and she allowed them to close once more, calling to mind the robed mould of Father Konstantin. She was never christened, nor was she raised in an overtly religious household, but just then, even the idea of a burial on sacred grounds constituted blasphemy. She cursed herself for thinking of him at such an inopportune time, imagining him somewhere overhead, looking down on her with stern judgement. If there were a world beyond the one she currently inhabited, certainly, he would not let her pass.

She dreamt of Uncle Leo, of his tattoos, suspecting he was reasonably skilled in the type of predicament she found herself in. Whether or not he was candidly involved in anything similar was unclear; granted, he must have, at least in some measure, seen and heard. She entertained the idea of telling him the whole rotten truth, for he would understand and know what to do next. On second thought, a secret was only a secret when left unspoken, and involving other parties, who may later give way to their own agendas, was unwise.

Dessa roused, this time in a cold sweat, hoping all was a vivid dream, yet the figurine she clasped tightly proved otherwise. The horror was far from over, and the night ahead promised an extra helping of dread. The night! It was far past nine, and she had to return to the scene of the crime this instant. Putting away the antelope, she shuddered at the lingering memory of her earlier vermin encounter.

"The rats!" she cried out abruptly in a voice so fiendish, it was unrecognizable to her as her own. A moment of clarity set in. "Indeed, it will be!" she spoke out loud, as a course of action so vile, and yet, so absolute dawned upon her. It was simpler than she originally had planned. She set to gathering the necessary supplies: a wet rag, some rope, and a few yards of old fabric. Tonight, the rats would be treated to a magnificent feast.

When Dessa neared the maintenance sheds, she was met with an unexpected, alarming surprise. The pack of strays, circling about the building earlier, was now interested in the hidden contents of the shrubbery. It was not about getting a meal, for they were generally well fed by the residents, but rather a question of territory that they presently took as their own. She clapped and hissed for them to get out; they growled and scowled in return, flashing their fangs. Had this continued any longer, she fretted of a potential audience appearing in the windows, or worse, on their balconies. The standoff lasted close to five minutes, until Dessa emphatically wielded a spading fork and, nicking with it one of the strays, dissuaded the rest of the pack from further confrontation. With a chorus of yelps, they scurried past the sheds, down the cobblestone path, and out of the courtyard.

Anxious to get on with it, she had to partake in yet another distraction, as fallen branches crackled under somebody's feet on the other side of the brick wall. Dessa stalled and listened closely. By the sound of it, the stranger stood directly across from her and, with the sudden quiet, was presumably aware of having given away his position. The wicket gate was not far off, and Dessa shivered at the frightening thought of this unknown taking initiative to explore the happenings this side of the barrier.

She counted the candidates. Aside from the bell tower monk responsible for lighting up the cathedral, the monastery grounds should have been deserted. The monk never trailed off course and stayed in the bell tower well after midnight, before shutting off the lamps for good, and retiring to his quarters. There was no reason for him to wander in these parts, and Dessa had a sneaking suspicion that he was still very much in the tower.

The waiting game went on. She dared not stir. The twigs rustled once more; light, cautious footsteps progressed along the wall and away from the wicket gate. She lent another minute. It was all too dangerous now. There was no chance to move the body in absolute silence, and she worried the stranger would return at the slightest hint of activity. She huddled, crossed her legs, and bided her time.

Half an hour later, convinced the danger had subsided, Dessa got to work. She spread out the fabric on the sand and, pattering through the brush, took hold of Sasha's ankles, dragging him onto the material. The task was not without difficulty. Unable to quit, mentally and physically exhausted, she swayed from side to side like a storm-battered leaf. Dessa did her best not to ogle the body and kept her eyes firmly on his lower extremities. She wrapped him in the fabric and tied the thick rope around his feet.

Taking hold of the rope and throwing it across her shoulder, she pulled the body in sporadic jolts toward the basement. Crossing the cobblestone path proved most tedious as Sasha's body bobbled and bounced; the uneven stones and their irregular deep crevices provided friction, slowing the process significantly. Getting to the doors required a trip down a set of steep stairs, and Dessa anticipated with horror every thump of the skull against the severe, unforgiving granite. The stairs never seemed so steep. On this night, they were colder, harder, and longer; the main path wider, its cracks down-reaching; the treetops higher, their branches more menacing. All was out of proportion, and every corner housed an insidious darkness.

In the corridor, she turned on the flashlight and, hooking it onto her belt, clumsily tugged the bulky mass in the direction of the garbage chutes. The bruxing and boggling of the rats grew louder with every advance. She pulled the body through the swinging doors, panting for air as her senses were ambushed by a nauseating spectrum of putrid slop and decay. Creatures scampered into the walls, others dashed under the trolleys, and some stuck around, unfazed by new company. The commotion and Dessa's swinging flashlight initiated a morbid dance of shadows. She limped around the doors, palming the walls, desperately searching for the light switch that turned out to be taped over and out of use. She would have to carry on as is.

Unwrapping the body, Dessa assumed it essential to remove all clothing and proceeded to do so with whirlwind speed. Her eyes burned from the biting scents; she could taste the muck on her tongue, and when she swallowed, it permeated deeper into her intestines. She was down to his underwear now, and with each pull, a wave of repulsive memories overwhelmed her mind. "Damned paedophile," she muttered under her breath, throwing the boxer shorts onto a growing heap of clothes. She rolled it into the fabric and tied it off with a rope, leaving the method of its disposal a worry for another occasion.

It may have been fitting to stay put and make sure those vile creatures took the bait, but Dessa could not stand it. She planned to come back the next night to check on their progress; and if, by twisted chance, he was found during the day, then so be it. Raskolnikov called this the pivotal time frame where the suspect was bound to make a mistake, to overlook a clue, and leave an incriminating piece of him or herself behind.

She was too tired to care. She grabbed the makeshift sack with Sasha's clothes and headed to the sheds. There, she scrubbed down the gardening tools, hoed patches of earth where he had bled out, and sifted the sand with newfound vigour. The air was pleasantly crisp and smelled of impending rain. She inhaled it hungrily over and over, concluding that it was the most intoxicating and liberating scent of the night.

Chapter 8

The after-hours of Dessa's hellish night yielded the longest and soundest sleep of her life. The clock struck six in the early evening, and the sun shifted out of view before she threw off the covers at last and headed into the kitchen to brew a hot cup of tea. While neither phone nor doorbell had rung once throughout the day, she expected Klara to drop in. By all estimations, Klara remained sore about yesterday's spat. To avoid fostering unnecessary resentment that could easily manifest suspicion elsewhere, Dessa had to negotiate a truce. She lifted the receiver and dialled her friend.

"Speaking," answered a lax male voice on the other end of the line.

"Good evening, Yakov. Is Klara around?"

"One moment." He cleared his throat for a pause. "Are you well?"

"Who, me?"

"Yes, you. Who else?"

"Why wouldn't I be?"

"You're on your own, are you not?"

Dessa deliberated.

"Don't sweat it, I won't squeal," he chuckled, handing over the receiver before Dessa could retort.

"What do you want?" said Klara.

"You shouldn't have told him."

"Well, I did."

"Are you coming over?" asked Dessa.

"Best not."

"Why not?"

"I'm busy."

"Doing what?"

"I can't talk."

"Wait!"

"Goodbye."

Dessa was beside herself. So be it, she thought, elbowing the telephone aside. She was not one to hold Klara's hand or baby her feelings. The call was her way of reaching out. Klara knew it and chose to uphold her silly vendetta instead. One spat had snowballed into a grudge toward their entire friendship, a bond that was not set up to function on equal terms from the very beginning. Dessa led, Klara followed, and this was by far the worst time for Klara to try and contest their arrangement.

Dessa passed the next hours watching the telly, making certain Klara did not change her mind and spring a surprise visit. When the cathedral lit up at nine o'clock, she was convinced the Feldblums were close to turning in, if they had not already done so. With a flashlight in hand, she listened closely for the affirmative silence of the elevator shaft. The coast was clear. She slipped out of her apartment and journeyed back inside the basement to check on the progress of what she resolved to be a foolproof, brilliant plan.

To her astonishment and utter horror, the body, now tinted shades of pale olive, lay virtually untouched. Shallow bite marks accented the toes, wrists, inner thighs and upper chest, yet there was little indication the creatures were any more interested in Sasha than in the other hoards of rubbish scattered about. He tasted vile even to the most indiscriminate vermin. If this was to be the final outcome, Dessa required a new course of action. Given another day, the body would be in no condition for transport, nor was she sure there was any strength left in her bones to drag him back out into the courtyard and possibly farther. He had to stay put, and were a carry-out imminent, it would have to be done in pieces.

In pieces. The words flickered in her mind with the dramatic lustre of a theatre marquee on opening night. Years ago, she lost her bearings at the Sunday market and had to zip through the back of a butcher's kiosk to spot her way out. Prime cuts of meat were mounted on the counter top with a crate of bloody oddities stashed underneath. The air was static and thick, rounding out the final hours of an unforgiving summer afternoon. The flesh smelled hot, sweet, close, vital, intense and, after a short while, uniquely nauseating. A row of stained hatchets glistened on the knife rack above her head. She would need one of them now, indubitably so.

It was her lone memory to draw on, and Dessa could not picture the task in front of her in any other way. Her limbs grew heavy again. Energy seemed to come in spurts, and the moment she over exerted herself physically, mentally, or emotionally, the crash would stream down like a mammoth waterfall, pendulating her fragile shape from wall to wall. She gathered what strength she had left and willed herself through the maze of corridors and up the winding stairs to the reassuring comfort of her vacant flat.

Once in the door, she foraged every shelf, drawer, and broom closet in search of an axe, and after coming up short, settled for an old, rusty meat cleaver discovered at random on the bottom tray of a kitchen cabinet. There was no contemplation of how, only a dead certainty that it had to be done. She would allow one more day and go back tomorrow evening. If there were no changes, she would have to chop up the corpse. Her mind shifted to the bloody butcher's crate as she slumped into the welcoming coolness of her bed linen and fell asleep.

⁂

The next morning, Dessa's first order of business was to do away with Sasha's clothes. They were crisp with stains, and merely burying them in the ground would attract strays chasing the scent of blood. Throwing them in the dumpster was a straightforward, effortless choice, primarily if the pieces were littered around the area. No good, she rationalized, for the vagrants that occasionally passed through these parts could discover the rags and make use of them. An investigation would be launched, drifters questioned, clothes seen, suspicion compulsory; infinite scenarios of things gone wrong, and she could spend hours, days hypothesising every possible blunder. Anything could trigger a foul-up. The duds had to stay put.

Dessa caught sight of Mother's hefty sewing scissors. After diligently cutting the evidence into thin strips of cloth, she turned on the gas stove, retrieved an empty sardine tin from the wastebasket, and pulled up a counter stool.

Blue flames licked the strips one by one as Dessa flung them in the tin before the heat could reach her fingers. A small ventilation window was perpetually unfastened, and whatever faint smell rose from the burn wafted straight through to the outside. With each shrivelled scrap, a clue vanished into thin air, its only remnant a wan string of withering smoke.

⁂

As deep nightfall blanketed the skies, Dessa travelled to the basement for what she swore would be the last time. The cathedral's lights had gone out hours ago. The clock neared three. She had stalled the inevitable long enough, as if wishing him away could do the trick, and when she walked in, he simply would not be there. Even in death, he waited, tormented.

Armed with the cleaver and a slew of used shopping bags, she passed through the narrow hallway and sheepishly entered the chute room. A silent gasp escaped her lips; she dropped the supplies. Her knees weakened and shook uncontrollably as she slid to the floor. Running her hands along the wall, Dessa grasped at it, feeling only the caked-on filth under her fingers. Ominous squeaks echoed throughout the room. She was immobile, quivering with fear. The body was gone.

"Impossible," she muttered, but the eyes did not deceive.

Instinctively, she crawled to the spot where Sasha lay just a day prior and poked at the flooring; it was clean. Terrified of the possibilities, she canvassed the area, scrutinizing every corner. There was no trace of the corpse anywhere.

Dessa was left with an entirely harrowing and seemingly improbable explanation. A stranger had trespassed on her cover-up, took the body, and tidied up the crime scene. She had an accomplice.

The air was warm; too warm, in fact, like a gymnasium after a spirited sports practice. Whoever was here just missed her or, quite conceivably, never left and was lurking, watching. Frightened out of her wits, she plucked her things off the floor and sprinted upstairs.

The remainder of Dessa's May Day holiday was spent under the covers. The elevator's trips became more frequent. People were coming home. Maybe one of them knew her secret; knew where she lived. Maybe one of them would ring the bell any minute now and expose her crime. She heard the elevator stall within reach as a pair of heels clicked closer and closer toward the front door. She identified the habitual fumbling of keys, a turn, and a snap, followed by a firm push. Mother was home.

Chapter 9

The dance recital drew near, and grand preparations forged ahead at maximum speed. New sets were erected in the gargantuan attic which served as the theatre's principal scene shop. During rehearsal breaks, curious pupils rode a private elevator to the fourth floor and admired the magical craftsmanship of what would soon turn into the ethereal world of Damsels of Laylavie Springs.

The scenery was in various stages of completion, making the woodworkers, plasterers, electricians, and painters all the more wizardly and captivating to observe. Rainbows of fabric rolls arrived hourly from the warehouse down the street, and the costumier wing echoed with the jangle of treadle sewing machines. Brochures, accentuated by freshly minted pocket calendars, were on display in the vestibule of the theatre and at exterior ticket counters. The idea was a roaring success, and passersby eagerly snapped up the complementary adverts.

Because the academic curriculum was officially over, the daily rehearsals became longer, starting as early as eight o'clock in the morning and going well past four in the afternoon. The dancers lived, dreamed, and breathed every routine. Frequently, they practised in the streets, in the metro, on the trams, at the market, at home, and in what few hours of sleep they managed to steal from time to time. The sacrifice was well worth it, for many viewed the recital, and more importantly, their part in it, as the utmost pivotal night of the year.

Djukin dropped in on the hour, demanding condensed reviews of all routines practised in that time frame. The troupes carried on splendidly, save for the shaky piano accompaniment that inadvertently threw many dancers off course.

Mistress Galina struggled with the new lad called upon to take over the piano duties after Sasha failed to show for work close to a week ago. He was said to board in a residence hall at the Conservatory that was systematically vacated for the summer. There were no traces of him there, although his meagre belongings did appear to stay put. No family was on record for contact, no friends came forward, and his employer at the porcelain boutique was equally unaware.

The production took so much time and energy that no one bothered to question his whereabouts, much less report him missing. His absence was assumed to be youthful negligence, and theatre heads swiftly contacted the Conservatory to inquire about a temporary replacement.

Their violent spat could not have occurred at a more opportune time. During the May Day holidays, no one cared to wonder where he was, thus, an entire week passed uneventfully. Then, at least another week passed before his employer would realise that something was amiss, speculating the circumstances of his departure to be dubious in nature.

The porcelain shopkeeper finally reported Sasha missing on the 22nd of May, aiding in the launch of an official investigation.

Dessa and Klara hurried to their morning rehearsal. Opening night of Djukin's production was mere days away, and the girls' nerves were acting up. They had not chatted much since their fallout, and when the opportunity did present itself at times like these, they were too consumed with thoughts of their looming performance to bother with small talk.

On this day, however, Klara broke their long-standing silence.

"What do you think happened to Sasha?"

Dessa's whole body gave way to an involuntary shudder, calling forth vivid imagery she had spent weeks desperately trying to suppress.

"I've no idea," she replied curtly. "He seemed quite the flake, so his sudden absence is not entirely surprising."

"Sounds like you may have been the last to see him."

"Why would you say that?"

"Well, you did have that engagement with him, and rumour is he has not been spotted since around that time."

"He stood me up."

"Oh? I was certain you met him."

"No, I waited, and he never came."

"That's strange," mumbled Klara to herself.

"Why is it strange?"

The girl shook her head and gave a weak smile, as if to demonstrate it was nothing, and there was no cause for alarm. Dessa was far from assured, and a tense, pulsating sensation took control of her limbs.

"I saw some men talking to the Mistress about him the other morning," continued Klara.

"What kind of men?"

"Detectives, I think. They weren't in uniform, definitely the brawny type, with worn leather jackets, chain smoking and swearing. The kind you see on the telly."

"What did they find out?"

"Not sure. The mistress was adamant that Sasha wouldn't disappear without notice and was decidedly not, as you put it, a flake."

Dessa detected an accusatory tone in her voice. Not only was Klara doubtful of their supposedly failed rendezvous, she clearly knew more about the matter than she cared to let on. Dessa clenched her fists, getting a firm grasp on herself. Her friend could not have seen anything that night. Technically speaking, it was impossible, simply because the Feldblums' balcony and windows faced the main street and not the courtyard.

She anticipated that, from this point forward, every conversation would need to be thought out well in advance and with extra care. Any ambiguity in her words or gestures could rouse distrust and lead to incrimination. The danger was in saying too much as it was in saying too little, in being overly curious and not curious enough. A fine balance had to be struck.

"Hmm... well, what do I know?" she concluded after a long pause, hoping to smooth over Klara's breeding uncertainty.

"He stood me up before, so I figured him for a flake, that's all."

"I do hope he turns up."

Dessa almost blurted out a trenchant "Why?" thinking better of it before it was too late. "I didn't gather you two were that close."

Klara did not respond. Silence befell them again.

Dessa snapped out of it with the aid of an abrupt, piercing screech. She found herself sitting on the edge of the trottoir, with Klara restlessly tugging on her jacket. People gathered round.

"She stepped out into traffic," someone hollered.

"Didn't even look!" added another reproachfully.

"What is wrong with you?" pleaded Klara. "He almost ran you over!"

"Almost, but no cigar," said Dessa drily and lifted up on her feet. She dusted herself off and slipped past the stopped cars as drivers looked on in amusement.

On the sidewalk, heads were shaking in disapproval. Klara thought it appropriate to curtsy before she dared catch up with her friend.

"Have you gone mad?" She was out of breath, chocking on her words.

"So, you deem me mad because I didn't anticipate a car? A bit harsh, wouldn't you say?"

"I just mean you haven't been yourself lately."

"Is that so? Goes for the both of us, then."

"I've no idea what you mean."

"Cut the act, Klara. I've been kind enough not to ask how or why you are even here," Dessa snapped, reaching the entrance to the costumier wing. "Friends tell each other everything, and frankly, you haven't said much since the casting. Yes, you are right in that something is nagging at my mind, and it is no more for your ears than your secrets are for mine, understood?"

She did not care to hear a rebuttal, if one was indeed coming, and darted through the doors, leaving Klara far behind. The outburst was principally staged for effect. Had Dessa dramatically conveyed the grievance she nursed against Klara's unusual secrecy, the focus on her own off-colour behaviour could momentarily shift. Sooner or later, her friend would talk, for she cherished Dessa's companionship too dearly to let the darkness come between them.

ॐ

On the mild Saturday evening of May 30th, the theatre's court hummed with enlivened discourse. Clusters of dolled-up women on the arms of polished gentlemen provided a heightened air of sophistication. Many were proud relatives of the night's performers, and although this was no classical production benefiting from prominent names, they carried on as if in attendance at Tchaikovsky's Swan Lake starring the likes of Maya Plisetskaya.

Groups of children lined up on the steps in anticipation as guides engaged in thorough head counts and confirmed seating arrangements printed on their tickets. The doors would open any minute now, allowing throngs of eager spectators to fill the foyer. Checking their mink shawls, trench coats, and umbrellas, excited masses would dispatch to the auditorium and its upper tiers. On this night, the theatre, capable of accommodating upward of 1,300 persons, would have every last seat accounted for with proud family members.

Backstage, dressing quarters buzzed with seamstresses hastily fitting dancers into their wardrobe. Hangers abundant with tulle, velvet, satin, and crêpe de Chine bedecked every doorway. Girls crowded at makeup stations, lining eyes, plumping lips, powdering cheeks, and fixing their headdresses. Boys in roles of animals and otherworldly creatures required assistance with complicated masks, wigs, and costume accessories. Some stretched alone in the corridors, anxious to take centre stage; others assembled in small groups and practised their routines one final time.

"Don't overdo it," barked the Mistress as she walked past, poking her head into rooms along the way.

In the midst of organized chaos, Dessa, Klara, and Inna were freshening up their faces at a shared vanity table in a separate room. The makeup artist, graciously assigned to the starring trio, had long gone, and was now tending to a group of male dancers in the hall, accentuating their brows and penciling in facial hair where there was none. The girls were made up flawlessly, but could not resist picking at their faces. While the other two fussed with lashes and sparkles, Dessa admired the brand-new pocket calendars, caringly pinning them to the mirror. June was theirs; July was dedicated to the female backup dancers; August's portrait comprised of the male ensemble posing proudly in embroidered tunics and sharovary.

"Ours turned out rather nice," Dessa said.

"Don't see what's so special about it," griped Inna. "They should've chosen a different pose."

"No, Dessa is right, this one is best," said Klara.

"Oh, of course, she is right. She is always right. I forgot, you're her loyal lapdog, isn't that so? How did you get this part, anyway, hmm?"

Klara was beyond reason. She accepted Dessa's open distrust and firmly believed it was within her friend's right to question the means by which she was here. She swore to work up the courage and tell Dessa every last bit in due time. Inna, on the other hand, was nobody passing off as somebody, riding on a dirty name and a long list of daddy's bribes. Supposing Klara may not have placed much higher on the moral ladder just then, she certainly was no lower than this spoon-fed diva.

No longer able to contain her emotions, she jerked Inna's shoulder and gave her a prompt slap across the face, retreating back to her seat in a jiffy. Her hand throbbed from the startlingly firm contact.

Inna roared in pain. Her cheek turned a deep shade of red; her eyes watered. She latched on to Klara's upper arms and gave her a violent jolt, thrusting the girl backwards onto the vanity. The counter rattled, the mirror shook. The girls wrestled, knocking down an array of brushes, creams, powders, and lights. The calendars soon followed. A bottle of rose water tipped and fell on the floor, spilling onto the trio's immaculate snapshot.

Having heard and seen all she cared to witness, Dessa interposed at last. "Quit it! Both of you," she said, picking up the soaked calendar. To her surprise, the colours did not leak and the cardstock kept its shape. She gingerly wiped it down, setting it aside.

A disconcerting quiet befell the trio as they surveyed the damage. An unanticipated chime of the first bell reverberated throughout every corner of the theatre. It was a quarter to seven, and they were expected on stage shortly.

"We'll have to clean this up later," Dessa asserted sombrely and exited the dressing room.

❧

The third and final bell rang at seven sharp; the melodic discord from the orchestra pit levelled off; the patrons' spirited chatter subdued. Wall sconces dimmed first; the stately Viennese chandelier followed. Some stirred in their seats, assuming a definitive posture of grace and earnest concentration. The curtains parted. The stage illuminated. The conductor raised his baton, and the performance commenced.

The first act portrayed the damsels of Laylavie Springs as angelic beings immersed in a life of harmonious togetherness with nature and its inhabitants. The stage sparkled with iridescent pastels, fluttering limbs, and a superior tromp l'oeil mural of a grassy meadow. Violoncellos and harps accentuated elegant, sweeping movements of the young dancers, who executed flawless chaînés, grand jetés, and fouettés. Djukin paced behind the scenes, gesturing at those closest to the curtains, marvelling at his own magnificence. Despite the leading trio's excellence, the corps de ballet stole the show with their ballabile. Beauty in numbers triumphed.

A half-hour intermission was scheduled after the first curtain drop, and Dessa caught a glimpse of Lady Rama in the first row as she hopped off stage. The woman looked downtrodden and solemn. Her semblance was in sharp contrast with and ill-suited for the vivacious atmosphere of the auditorium's roaring crowd. Deafening applause engulfed her from all sides, yet she remained stiff with her legs crossed to the right, hands fixed at the waist, and head tilted slightly downward.

At a glance, Dessa detected a pair of strange figures two rows back of the pit. Husky and oafish, the men stood out, regardless

73

of their size and demeanour, for the casual dress they obliviously sported clashed with the rich, tailored attire that was par for the course. Immediately, she drew on Klara's description of those "brawny type" detectives and concluded it must have been them. Why were they here? Surely, out of all the places Sasha frequented, studied and worked, this could not be the most suspicious site for investigation. The detectives already came to talk to the staff privately and were now at the actual recital watching, waiting. Watching whom? Waiting for what? Dessa's sheer curiosity trumped burgeoning fears of exposure.

ఇ

The buffet was open and serving. Lady Rama capped off the long winding line in hopes of acquiring a glass of brandy and some marmalade fruit slices. The Opera's café bar was renowned for its fine selection of spirits, desserts, and cold platters, with patrons willingly shelling out extra cash to indulge in the mere novelty of their purchase. She was well aware of the pursuers who paid her a visit last week and claimed to be satisfied with the account she gave. Yet, they continued to stalk her. She caught sight of them in her building, at the butcher's, and later the Conservatory. The men invariably kept their distance. They had no substantial questions and no substantial leads, making Lady Rama a key interest out of simple necessity for a suspect and to save face in an already overburdened precinct.

A colleague of theirs, who happened to be Rama's former client, provided the detectives with an off-the-record exposé on her unconventional lifestyle. Because she was painted as a woman of loose morals, vast experience, and lewd inclinations, the detectives latched on as soon as an unnamed source at the Conservatory confirmed an illicit affair that Rama carried on with Sasha on a fairly prolonged basis. The age difference was scandalous as is, and it was quite possible for the lovers to have a quarrel, perhaps about the nature of her services for others or

74

his jealousy about the long list of suitors. Admittedly, the theory was paper-thin and, if true, did not directly incriminate her in his disappearance. Yet, it was more than the detectives could come up with otherwise, and so their futile pursuit continued.

Lady Rama was served her drink with a bowl of candies and sauntered to an open bistro table. The first bell rang. Savouring the melting citrus wedges on her tongue, she eavesdropped on animated exchanges between families of young performers as they hailed Foma Djukin and his lofty creative vision. Rama knew Djukin well and thought him a maladroit fruit with a penchant for hackneyed storytelling. The production was indeed spectacular, but no thanks to his efforts. The real visionaries were in the pit, on stage, above it, and behind it. It was the dancers, the craftsmen of sets, costumes, and music that turned a painfully trite concept into a night worthy of praise. No matter, she thought, for the papers would print his name tomorrow without due salute to anyone else.

The intermission passed quickly, and the second bell sounded much sooner than expected. Refreshed patrons strutted leisurely toward the auditorium with bellies full of drink and cheer. Rama finished her brandy and headed inside, mindful of the hulking duo trailing behind.

❧

A theatre attendant hoofed about the stage, checking on the craftsmen and their progress. If changes in lighting and scenic design were complete, she would ring the last bell. Those who snuck in for a speedy chat with the dancers were ushered out and asked to return to their seats.

The second act had a tenebrous start. Goblins and witches invaded Laylavie Springs, chasing out the damsels and their forest allies. The brass section soared with trumpets, horns, and trombones, providing stirring melodies to amplify the danger and dread of the spooky intruders. The story called for uncommon contemporary choreography alien to the audience's classically conditioned eyes, and they gazed in awe at the fluidity of these unusual techniques as dancers executed deliberate falls to the ground and then rose sporadically, contorting their bodies into improvisational stances.

The closing march was one for the books, uniting all of the troupes at centre stage. They sizzled with forte and drew fervent applause from electrified spectators. Families of performers would later boast that this was no ordinary children's recital, but a full-on extravaganza showcasing the future talent of Kiev's prestigious dance academy.

Multiple curtain calls maintained a drawn-out standing ovation, and when the general public finally dawdled toward the exits, families sprung backstage to congratulate their young. The leading trio's dressing room was crowded with the Feldblums, Mister Dvorkin with his current sleazy arm candy, Shurik, and Mother. Dvorkin shamelessly lauded Inna as the best of the three and presented her with a pair of emerald earrings. Yakov was engrossed in taking photographs of Klara with her parents, and Dessa clung to Shurik, waiting for the mob to disperse. She heard a familiar voice in the corridor, and a wave of jubilance swept through her veins.

"Papa Carlo!"

She sprinted into the hallway and scrunched tightly into the old man's torso.

"You were simply darling," he opined. "What a triumph, the finest damsel of them all."

Intrigued, Shurik and Mother popped out of the dressing room; introductions ensued. Shurik instantly embraced the veteran photographer, puppet maker, and stagehand, more commonly known to the public as Arkady Semyonovich Nazarov. While the elders chatted each other up, Mother headed out for a breath of fresh air. Klara tugged on Dessa's bodice, bidding her

76

farewell as she and her family left the dressing room. Inna's party followed shortly.

Delirious at the prospect of brief repose, Dessa slipped back inside, lounging on a settee crammed with masks and costumes. She propped her feet up on the vanity, reached for the pocket calendar, and took a big whiff. The cardstock was doused with the scent of roses. She threw her head back and scanned the masks. The goblin was most menacing, its expression twisted into a permanent, roguish grimace. Dessa gulped as chills ran down her spine. The mask was triggering a dreadful flashback.

Sinking in the settee, Dessa rewound her memory to the third night. Reliving her decision to undergo the unthinkable, she sketched out the winding stairs, drew in the stuffy air of the basement corridor, and felt the grime-covered walls on her fingertips.

To this day, the identity of her accomplice was cloaked in mystery. No contact, no blackmail, no body. There were pockets of time where Dessa breathed easy, but sobering reality was never far behind. Sooner or later, the co-conspirator had to show himself.

Chapter 10

Detectives Chuchin and Komarovsky moseyed along Ril'sky Lane in no rush to enter the station. Partnered close to five years, the duo had seen a noteworthy surge in missing persons during the turbulent season of change and "opportunity." Nearly a third of those reports were later confirmed as unlawful emigration, and though a vast majority of the remaining cases were undoubtedly criminal, it was now commonplace to assume a permanent leave of absence had the relatives and friends of the missing gradually abandoned their cause for a search. The way the detectives figured it, if those concerned pestered the staff on a regular basis, then it was fitting to sound the alarm. Had the visits subsided, the folks likely got word from their missing parties, who were now safely in a foreign land or overseas.

After months of investigating, however, the matter of Sasha Bandura was at a standstill. The probe already got off to a shoddy start, because for two whole weeks no one bothered to report the chap missing. When the shopkeeper of the porcelain boutique, where Bandura laboured on occasion, finally came in and filed a report, whatever leads and evidence there were had long vanished.

Chuchin and Komarovsky were given the case as a form of busywork after a routine drug raid went awry. They fell out badly with the chief over their unorthodox, boorish methods of interrogation and, as punishment, were temporarily downgraded to sort through files of the disappeared. The stint had long been over, but this last case perturbed Komarovsky ever since he found it on his desk. Neither man had a great eye for detail, was exceptionally in tune with his senses, nor harboured enough patience and expertise necessary for this line of work. The duo frequently relied on their burly appearance to extract information, gather evidence, and intimidate witnesses. Yet, with Bandura, there were no real suspects to interrogate and no clues to suggest foul play. All they had was a hunch based on Komarovsky's nagging feeling of insufficiency. The shopkeeper was no longer persistent with inquiries. Having lost an easily replaceable employee, he had no personal investment in the young fellow. Bandura showed no signs of family, friends, or acquaintances. Those who lived across the hall in his dorm could not even remember what he looked like, painting a vague picture of a quiet, forgettable boy whose only notable interactions were with Miss Ramazanova and the little girls at the dance academy. That slight bit struck Komarovsky as incredibly odd; something was off, he was sure of it, but neither he nor his partner possessed the mental capacity to figure out just what, precisely, was off kilter.

"I think the kid was up to no good," said Komarovsky, lighting a cigarette.

"Well, he is missing, so I would guess as much," replied a listless Chuchin.

They stopped in front of a towering banking centre with exhaustively waxed windows, and Chuchin, preoccupied with his own reflection, was nervously stroking his receding hairline and rapidly thinning crown.

The men were close in age, both entering their early forties, and while Komarovsky could not be bothered with his outward appearance, Chuchin took every opportunity to scrutinize his aging body.

"It's all going to shit," he frowned.

"He's got to have another place somewhere," continued Komarovsky to himself.

"What are you on about?"

"You, cretin. He must have a different flat somewhere. The dorms were not his primary residence, that's why we didn't find anything, get it?"

"No, I don't get it. Because if he did have another place, someone else would have come forward already, like a landlady, for instance."

Komarovsky scratched his brow; both theories were correct.

"You have a point. Let's go through what is left at the dorm."

"Again?"

"We weren't looking for the right clues last time."

"Didn't they toss his junk?"

"The furniture, yes. The rest is boxed up in their basement. Let's have another look, shall we?"

Chuchin shrugged his shoulders and started toward the parking garage. They had more pressing cases to worry about, with stacks of them waiting on their desks, but he also knew his partner. Bandura's case, no matter how trivial, had gotten hold of Komarovsky, and there would be no give until they saw it through. The twosome climbed into their well-kept, cream-coloured GAZ-24 Volga and sped out of the station's gateway, heading straight for the Conservatory.

❧

The contents of the boxes did not generate a great deal of pertinent information. There were schoolbooks, records, sheet music, a few notepads, and some clothes.

"What are we looking for, Komar? There's nothing here."

"Take a notebook and start reading."

"It's just lecture notes."

"No matter, keep reading."

A noticeably frustrated Chuchin flipped loudly through endless pages of musical theory and historiography.

"This is a waste of time," he said, hurling the notepad back in the box. "Keep this up, and we'll fall out with the chief again, only this time around we're going straight to paper pushing."

Komarovsky smacked his lips and kept on skimming the notes. A student, sorting crates of sheet music nearby, took special interest in the notepads.

"Whoa, those are neat!"

"How do you mean?" inquired Komarovsky.

"Well, they are handmade, leather-bound, and use heavy paper stock. Quite expensive, really, and very sought after. I know of maybe two stores that carry them."

"That rare, hmm?"

Komarovsky asked the fellow for directions and, with an upbeat strut in his step, exited the basement.

"We have ourselves a lead!"

"He can't be serious," pondered Chuchin, falling a step behind, desperately searching his coat for a pack of smokes.

❧

The first shop, standing on the edge of the Right Bank, yielded nothing, and the duo was quickly off to their second destination, situated much farther across the river. Upon arrival, they noted the area was a low-cost student haven, and Komarovsky surmised it to be the place where they would surely get on the trail of this elusive young man. After engaging in a brisk tête-à-tête with the shopkeeper, the detectives were made aware that a man fitting their description did indeed, at one time, frequent these parts and was rumoured to have shared a small space with a much older, shady character who resided in a rundown apartment block around the corner.

They gave thanks and departed the shop, heading to the next site of interest. The self-congratulating smirk on Komarovsky's mug was driving Chuchin positively mad. His partner was just an inch too sure of himself, acting as if this were an investigative breakthrough when, in reality, it was no more than a case of pure dumb luck.

The building was in worse shape than originally described, and the detectives were wary of the idea that anyone, aside from an incidental vagrant, could lodge in such squalid conditions. Most of the complex looked empty. There was no elevator, and the staircase was missing all of its handrails.

"There is no way he lived here," said Chuchin.

"I agree. He lived at the dorms, carrying on with his business here."

"What kind of business?"

"We are about to find out."

They started up the stairs, careful to skirt strewn-about eggshells, bits of rotting food, and pools of what smelled like animal or, equally likely, human urine.

Chuchin pulled out a wrinkled handkerchief to cover his face. His eyes were starting to water. Out of the dozen or so apartments in the building, just three were visibly occupied. Komarovsky took initiative and visited with those occupants who were not too drunk or strung out to aid in his inquiries. He was told the older man and his boyish companion nested in the garret. No one had seen either of them for weeks, if not months. During early June, however, some noted a foul odour emanating from the upstairs. Naturally, nobody bothered to investigate. It was now mid-July.

Komarovsky turned to Chuchin with a knowing squint. "Let's go."

82

"Where to?"

"I think we are about to seal this case!"

He propelled to the attic with an inappropriately perverse level of delight. The front door was ajar. He pushed it open with his boot and unceremoniously marched in.

Chuchin lingered in the doorway, uncomfortable with his partner's impulsive bravado, as well as the speed and ease with which everything was neatly falling into place after laborious months of nothingness.

Faced with an unnerving quiet, he wondered just what kind of a grisly scene they had stumbled upon. With a deep inhale he trudged inside.

Komarovsky stood in the corner, his face hidden by severe shadows of the inadequately lit room. Chuchin gathered him to look rather pale. The enthusiasm he was fired up with mere moments ago had all but flushed from his body.

"A dog," he said.

"Pardon?"

"A dead dog."

Chuchin scanned the room and neared a loo table under which he saw a badly decomposed animal carcass. Komarovsky was beside himself, and Chuchin rejoiced quietly, relieved that the case had not come together in an eerie bout of perfection. He was well aware of their lacking investigative capabilities, and a mystery of this calibre solved by a stupendously accidental string of good fortune spelled out a bad omen of sorts. While his partner was spellbound by and thoroughly absorbed in Bandura's disappearance, Chuchin, in a spontaneous change of heart, was now more than ever hesitant to pursue the case any further.

"Have your feet turned to stone?" said Komarovsky.

"Huh?"

"You've been gawking at it for a good two minutes now. Get cracking, we have a lot to comb through."

On the contrary, there really was nothing to rummage. In the tiny dwelling stood a single bed, a nightstand, and the loo table. A chair and a portable gas stove propped up haphazardly on a tottering commode near the entrance passed for a makeshift kitchen. There was no lavatory. Jumbles of newspapers littered the floor, most of them soaked with more urine. Komarovsky headed for the nightstand, and Chuchin decided to take the commode.

"Damn thing is locked. Give me your screwdriver."

Chuchin reached in the inner pocket of his blazer and pitched his partner a miniature flathead screwdriver. Komarovsky then fished out a paperclip, straightened it out, and proceeded to fumble with the lock. Chuchin thought it a comical sight, as there was no audience and dispensing a rough slog would suffice. As per usual, this guy needed to make a whole show of it. Annoyed, he delved into the drawers of the commode, their contents limited to a handful of dirty rags, condoms, and a stash of gay pornography.

"So, they were queers?"

"Well, not quite," echoed Komarovsky, who had pried open the nightstand and was heedfully sorting its contents.

"What've you got?"

"Kids, Chuch. All kids."

Chuchin approached the nightstand and knelt beside his partner. The drawer was full of photographs of prepubescent kids in various states of undress, most of them girls.

"What you found in the commode is the old man's junk. This here is Bandura's."

"I don't get it, were they working together, or not?"

"I'd guess the old fart is strictly queer, and the missing kid was his rent boy. By the looks of it, Bandura was game for just about anything. Maybe he did this shit for cash and the girls for pleasure."

"And Ramazanova?"

"She's the piece of the puzzle that doesn't quite fit. Sure, she's into some kinky stuff that he may gladly partake in, but for a guy who's into either old fags or little kids, she kind of misses his preferred demographic."

"Maybe the pervert doesn't discriminate."

"Or maybe Ramazanova knows a lot more than she's letting on. We should pay her another visit."

"On what grounds?"

"I don't know, Chuch, find something. For now, we need to identify the children."

With newfound evidence, Chuchin was nurturing an idea.

"What if it's someone from their families? Say he diddles these kids, and a sibling or a parent finds out. The prick is as good as dead."

"A very plausible scenario."

"Not that I'd blame them."

"Neither would I," said Komarovsky, raking the photographs into a heap. "We still have to investigate. Have you got a bag?"

Chuchin shook his head and glanced about the room for an alternative, handing Komarovsky dated sheets of newspaper.

"Here, wrap it in these."

Skimming the subjects, a flash of familiarity triggered his senses. Chuchin leaned in for closer inspection.

"Wait a minute, that one there," he pointed to a picture of a little girl, maybe ten years of age, thin, bushy browed, dark haired, fair skinned, and wide eyed. "I've seen her before, so have you."

He stood there, frozen in place, with his partner showing no signs of recognition.

"Well, cut the suspense already! Seen her where?"

"The Opera House, dipshit. Laylavie Springs, she was one of the leads."

85

Komarovsky studied the photograph and slapped his forehead.

"Jesus Christ, we are onto something big here, Chuch!"

"So, now what?"

"We go see the girl, question her ever so delicately."

"And the old queer?"

"To hell with him, and to hell with this dump. Let's blow this trap."

"As you wish."

The twosome withdrew from the attic, scurried down the stairs, onto the street, and out of sight.

Chapter 11

After a long week of May Day holidays, the dance recital, and well into the summer heat, Mother signed up for an evening class of English lessons on the recommendation of a close female friend. The lessons were promoted in a local advert paper and promised instantaneous results on account of regular correspondences with native speakers, the access to which the school would readily provide free of charge.

With a fresh hobby stretching her schedule, Mother was rarely home before supper. Many a time, Dessa was left to her own devices. She deemed Mother's lessons too cheap for the miracles they endorsed and took the instructors for crooks, as they had no set curriculum or even a textbook their so-called "students" could follow. She supposed it to be some sort of an elaborate scam, and on the dreaded day when Mother made her come along, she witnessed a masquerade of thirty-something women trying desperately to find themselves a foreign mate.

Dessa thought something was amiss when week after week not a single male attended the class, and soon after, the nature of the lessons exposed the school as a booming marriage agency. Initially, the women were encouraged to practice their newfound language skills by writing short essays about themselves to no one in particular. With time, the letters became directed at specific individuals and were mailed out on a regular basis. State-monitored pen pal programs were not unusual, even during the gravest of Soviet times, and encouraged citizens of all ages to build ties with outsiders, so long as those outsiders remained inside the Iron Curtain.

These pen pals, however, were of an entirely different breed. For one, they were always men and always American. They were older, single, and looking.

Dessa sympathized with the dire state of romantic affairs in their own country, but wondered why anyone else outside of it would want to come here and find love. Nevertheless, in a matter of weeks, their letterbox filled with missives from dozens of potential admirers, and Mother spent hours on the telephone weighing the suitors with her female friends, dividing them into categories of those who were eligible, those who were not, and those who were yet undecided.

Essentially, the same principle was applied as when shopping around for a new refrigerator or vacuum cleaner. One looked at the different brands, compared prices, analysed durability, checked the warranty, and made a purchase. The popular opinion suggested that it was men who purchased, hence the quickly adopted slang of acquiring a "mail-order bride." However, it was really the woman who screened and later chose her husband. It was she who had a choice between candidate A and candidate B, whereas the male suitors were usually content to settle for any woman who took good care of her outward appearance and exhibited the slightest interest in them. And so, the bulk of the summer was spent auditioning male applicants for the role of Mother's next promising spouse.

About a week before Dessa's birthday, Mother made the decision to share the men's profiles with her daughter, because the candidates were now decisively narrowed down to three. All men were entering their forties, divorced, and childless. There was Robert Montgomery, an insurance clerk from Santa Barbara, California; Chuck Bedford, a cattle rancher from Roscoe, Montana; and Stevie Driscoll, an antique shop owner from Richmond, Virginia.

Dessa did not have a preference one way or another. She was partial to Chuck because he wore cowboy hats and had spurs on his boots; she liked Robert because his city of residence reminded her of everyone's favourite soap opera; and Stevie had the appeal of someone with a store full of toys and nifty knick-knacks.

When Mother was at work, Dessa regularly read and reread the suitors' letters. Her English was more sophisticated, and she hoped to catch something in the men's words or tone that was, perhaps, undetectable to a novice reader. She was curious about their intentions, because unlike most of the women at the marriage agency, Mother was already with child, a common turn-off to someone who had their pick of the litter. Yet, these men were persistent and, with every new correspondence, were selling Mother a dream Dessa feared was too good to be true.

All were boasting of financial security, but the Faustov clan had yet to fall on hard times. Dessa guessed that being rich overseas meant something entirely different and more grandiose in comparison to the comfortable lifestyle she currently enjoyed. America was painted as the land of freedom and opportunity, and the girl also pondered if American "opportunity" was quite contrary to the favourable circumstances enjoyed by many in their own new era of independence. Of course, most women at the agency were looking for just that after leading lives of ongoing financial instability and personal hardship. They were tired of deadbeats and drunks, low wages, and gender discrimination, with Mother unfit for the bill of a "typical" mail-order bride. Dessa concluded that, for her, the fundamental draw of these unions was, indeed, the marriage itself. She must have been fed up with the solitary lifestyle her family situation afforded. For local available men who were up to standard, she was no more than a divorced single mother well past her prime, whereas for a select few overseas, she remained a valuable commodity.

She was smitten by having acquired so many options in a relatively short period of time, for romantic choice was never a practice she freely indulged in. Then, there was the obvious cultural draw of the unknown, the vastness of the land, the difference in courtship, and the championing of true family values. When musing about the suitors in this new light, Dessa, too, grew fond of the idea of la dolce vita. She dreamed of one day splitting her time between two great lands, spending the summers overseas, and later reciting her adventures in the schoolyard to a throng of craving and ever-envious classmates. The foreign fantasy was taking hold.

Chapter 12

The summer of' '92 was capped off with Dessa's triumphant twelfth birthday celebration. With the murderous spring all but forgotten, her eleventh year passed faster than the last, and she had a sinking feeling the next would pass even quicker. The day's festivities wrapped up in the late afternoon, and Mother, who was in unusually high spirits, allowed Dessa to slip out and spend time with her dear friend Klara. She suspected Mother's favourable disposition was the result of an unforeseen, congratulatory phone call from Chuck, who rang in the early morning to send his best wishes and proceeded to chat her up for a good half an hour. Out of her three chosen finalists, he was the only one to do so, and Mother read the tender gesture as an auspicious sign for potential marital bliss.

Dessa popped out of the apartment building and rushed to a nearby park where Klara instructed them to meet. She was there at present, waiting patiently on a bench at the far end of the gardens. The girls exchanged pleasantries, and Dessa was granted an elegantly wrapped parcel.

"More Dostoyevsky?"

"Oh dear, n—no, that was—"

"Don't fret, Klara. I'll be delighted if it is."

The package yielded a vivid, Khokhloma-painted jewellery casket, and Dessa's eyes twinkled at its sight.

"Incredible! What a fantastic offering. You shouldn't have. It's much too opulent."

"I want you to have it, keep in it what you will."

Her tone was decidedly eerie and final, and the girls spent the next minutes surveying the cracks in the pavement, unsure of how to broach the subject both so ardently wanted to discuss.

"Remember those detectives from the Opera House?" Klara asked at last.

"Sure, the brawny types."

"I haven't said anything to you about it for quite some time. Last month they came to see me."

"Oh?"

"They questioned my whole family."

"About Sasha? Jeez, those clowns must have been really strung up for leads. I figured they'd give it a rest ages ago."

"Well, as it turns out, aside from the dorms, he had another place somewhere on the Left Bank."

"How cliché for a hooligan. What did they find?"

"Other than some photographs, not much, it seems."

"Photographs?"

"Of me, among others—"

"What others?"

"I'm not too sure. Other girls, other boys. What's for certain is that he took them all."

"Hmm, boys? Even viler than I'd imagined," Dessa said and quickly caught herself. "How many?"

"Dozens, I'd say. They showed me a lot of them, hoping I could help identify the others. But, I couldn't."

Dessa was peeved to hear the detectives, who unquestionably had bigger fish to fry, were still pursuing the case after all this

92

time. At any rate, Klara's latest reveal cemented her belief that the fateful and merciless actions she took back in May were all but mandatory to rid the world of this monstrous being. As a matter of fact, knowing all the police knew about Sasha's revolting pastime, it was a wonder anyone even bothered to continue the search. "Good riddance," they should have said and tipped their hats.

"Don't worry, yours wasn't there," Klara said knowingly.

"Why would it be?"

"Didn't he take pictures of you, too?"

"No. Never. Not that I am aware of, anyway."

"Hold on, didn't you two– didn't he–?" Klara trailed off and lowered her eyes.

"Didn't we what?"

Dessa knew exactly what she was getting at, promising herself to tell no one and say nothing that even remotely hinted at her and Sasha's troubling liaisons. Klara was looking for assertion. Waiting for Dessa to admit that she, too, suffered abuse at his hands was a way to tackle her own feelings of shame in the comfort of miserable togetherness. But Dessa would not budge, so she let it be.

"Worst of all," Klara continued, "they suspect Yakov may have done something bad."

This was the real bombshell. Dessa's body quivered as a blazing shockwave travelled through her extremities. Of all the people she considered as her accomplice, Yakov never crossed her mind. Could it be that, on the night in question, it was he who covered her tracks and saved her from inevitable exposure and incrimination? Was it he who bore witness to her crime? The suggestion was more plausible now than any other, yet, there was no definitive proof and no satisfactory explanation of how he came to know. Was he passing by the courtyard, or did he make the grisly discovery later in the basement? If so, why was he there and how could he guess it was her doing? Did he already know what Sasha was up to and, therefore, took matters into his own hands to protect the girls? Protecting Klara was obvious, but why Dessa? Unless, of course, he thought it were Klara who committed the crime.

Absurdity! There were too many loose ends and unanswered questions. She had to keep calm.

"Do you believe he did, Klara?"

"I don't know. I mean, I don't think so. He was hopping mad, claiming he knew nothing of it until they presented him with the evidence."

"Sounds fair."

"Those goons trailed him at first. He hasn't spotted them around in a good while."

"Maybe, they actually found themselves a more credible lead or, better yet, dropped the whole thing."

"I doubt it. The one detective, Mister Komarovsky, he was really hung up on the case. Probably still is."

Dessa made a mental note of a certain Komarovsky.

"You know what Yakov said was truly strange? The detectives mentioned Lady Rama on numerous occasions."

"Rama? Why would she be involved?"

"I haven't a clue. They asked Yakov if he ever paid her visits."

"What kinds of visits?" Dessa inquired, pretending she knew nothing of Rama's long list of suspected suitors.

"After some asking around, they've taken her for a–, well, I don't know if I believe it, they said she was a–"

"A whore?"

Klara throbbed involuntarily at the unforgiving sharpness of the word. Nodding in agreement, she squirmed uncomfortably in her seat.

"If they asked Yakov about it, that means Sasha was seeing her, too. That pig got around well."

Dessa deduced that on the night of the recital the goons were keeping an eye on Rama, who did look rather sour and, in all likelihood, was entirely aware of their presence.

"Tell me truthfully, Dessa, do you think he is dead?"

"Why? Would you like him to be?"

"I never said that."

"I know, so would you?"

"I don't wish death on anyone."

"No? Not even murderers, thieves, or paedophiles? Because that's what he was, Klara."

"You know, there were times he seemed genuinely kind."

"Pfft! A mere ploy used to lure his gullible prey."

"So, you are happy he is gone, then?"

"I wouldn't say happy is the most appropriate word." No, the appropriate word was thrilled, elated, or ecstatic.

The girls sat in the park well into dusk, enjoying the warmth of a late August evening as the sweetly paralyzing aroma of the gardens' last phlox blossoms pulsed through still air.

"I should head home," said Klara. "I'm glad we talked."

"And I may stay a while longer. Thank you, for coming out and for the wonderful present. I do love it so."

She squeezed Klara's palm and watched her walk down the path under the flickering street lamps as her fragile figure blended in with the shadows and was lost in the hovering darkness of the night.

Intoxicated by the gardens' array of fragrances, Dessa felt a sudden wave of fatigue and numbness. Her body was plummeting into a trance, and she dared to give into it ever so briefly, before a familiar crackle stirred her out of the abyss. She sat upright and scanned the area, seeing no one. Sinking into her seat, she leaned back and began to drift. The crackle persisted, this time farther down the path. Dessa wondered if Klara was coming back, or if a dog had gotten loose on a routine walk, knowing full well it was neither. The same crackle she heard the night of the murder across the wall was now haunting her here. She perceived the sound on many lonesome occasions. It was distinctive, elusive, and taunting. If it were a mirage, she discerned not its underlying message. There was no guilt, no real fear, and only intense curiosity.

Dessa gathered her gift and willed herself to move forward. She passed the gardens and took an extended route around the neighbourhood before entering her apartment building. To prolong the surprisingly wondrous solitude, she opted for the stairs instead of the elevator. There was movement on the top floors, and she thought little of it, until its distinctiveness and elusiveness seeped downward. Dessa slowed her steps and studied the upper levels of the stairwell, waiting intently on the stranger to make a move. She pressed on, trudging past the third landing, and then the fourth.

A door opened up above, and a boisterous group of what sounded like drunken partygoers called up the elevator. As it whooshed past to the fifth floor, she realized whoever was up there would take the elevator as well, for there was no other way down except to walk straight through her. Ignited by the prospect of confrontation, Dessa shot up the steps. She had him now, whoever he was. At that moment of sheer certainty, she tripped over and sank to the floor. People were piling into the cabin, the doors drew shut, and the elevator went down. Dessa rubbed her bruised knee and searched for the object that so violently halted her efforts. A shoddy broomstick, usually kept in the garbage chute enclosure, lay near her feet. She reasoned it to be an accident, a rather convenient one at that, for the idea of deliberate harm made this already tense cat and mouse game all the more perverse.

She looked up the remaining steps where the stranger stood just minutes ago. Something very delicate and small gleamed at

96

from the top at the landing. She crawled closer and instantly recognized the figurine. It was the savannah elephant, the last and most extravagant piece to complete her safari. There was no note, no message, only the lone artifact. Was this a peace offering or a taunt? Nobody, not even Klara, knew about her porcelain collection or that it was Sasha who provided her with all of the pieces.

It hit her that if it were, in truth, Yakov's doing, he would not be at home then, but wandering about, biding his time to ensure a safe, undetected return. She plunged down the stairwell to the third floor and stopped short of ringing Klara's doorbell. It was getting late, and she had no legitimate excuse to be bothersome at this hour. Pressing her right ear to the door, she slowed her breathing, and listened intently. Faint voices trailed through the apartment, and she was unable to decipher if Yakov was one of them.

"Hello, Dessa," whispered a deep male voice behind her. The girl spun round, dropped her jewellery casket, and let out a vehement scream. Yakov stood on the landing, having silently taken the stairs. The lanky young man towered above her as she reached to the floor in his shadow. Heads popped out of a nearby flat. Yakov motioned them to retreat inside.

"Nothing to see here," he said and crouched beside Dessa. "Let me help you with that. I didn't mean to frighten you, please, forgive me."

"It's fine, I just wanted to thank Klara once more for my generous present. Seems I better do so tomorrow."

She awkwardly swept up the casket with its wrapping paper and ribbon and raced past him toward the staircase.

"You forgot something," he said in a tone so diabolical, it sent shivers down her spine.

As she turned around, he was already upon her, extending the porcelain figurine.

"You're lucky it didn't break," he grinned. "A generous present, indeed."

"Oh, this isn't–" she stopped herself short of playing into the trap. "Y–yes, thank you. It's quite lovely. Please, pass on my regards to Klara."

"Will do," he said and placed his hands in his pockets, keeping an eye on her as she treaded upstairs.

Chapter 13

Yakov Feldblum pushed a stacked, wobbly book cart through the library's basement archives, hoping to sort the material fast enough to make it home in time for supper. A plate would be set aside for him regardless, but he was a family-oriented young man and loved spending time at the table chatting up his parents and teasing his little sister.

Admittedly, ever since the goons from the station dropped in uninvited and soiled the Feldblum household with their smut, suppertime chatter left something to be desired. If he were a sure suspect, they knew precisely how and where to reach him without making a show of it. Instead, the pompous one, Komarovsky, thought it appropriate to involve the whole family and humiliate Klara. Spreading those filthy photographs along their dinner table almost made Yakov vomit. They spoke as if it were a sensitive matter, with the true goal of provoking a reaction from the relatives. The twosome questioned Klara ever so delicately, hanging on her every word like it held great significance; but what they really hoped for was an involuntary outburst, a twitch, a shake, or a look from Yakov to determine if he was harbouring any guilt of his own.

Although the young men did not share the same studies or faculty and were nodding acquaintances at best, Yakov and Sasha kept cordial with each other. The two were close in age, and Sasha often came to the Bibliotheca for research or to pass the time between courses.

It was a reference library, and all activity had to be conducted on the premises, allowing Yakov to track his shy peer more diligently. Sasha was forever alone and focussed on his work. There were days where he simply sat at his desk with a soaring pyramid of unopened books and stared at an invisible spot of his choosing.

He was a peculiar character, and Yakov found him compelling, if for no other reason than his ambiguity and elusive nature. The Conservatory, the Opera House, and the Braga Lyceum were all elite, tight-knit academic establishments, yet Sasha seemed exceptionally out of place wherever he went. This was not to say he was too foolish or untalented, but his behavioural oddities alienated him from his peers and colleagues, further fuelling Yakov's interest.

Cataloguing the last sheaf of papers, he was reminded of the first instance when his interest in Sasha morphed from the purely theoretical into an active physical pursuit. It happened earlier that year on a biting winter evening in late January when Yakov was on his way home from a study group. The snowfall was heavy, and those caught unawares hung their heads low. Yakov aimed his focus at the path in front of him and steadily marched on until his shoulder grazed an oncoming pedestrian. Apologetic, he raised his head to make amends, only to see a familiar face zoom past without notice. It was Sasha Bandura, who did not recognize or even acknowledge his peer, for he was in a dishevelled state and looked to be in an inflexible hurry. Right then, a deep-seeded hankering for gamble persuaded Yakov to deviate from his course and track Sasha in a potentially

100

risky venture. It could have led nowhere, adding up to a drawn-out stroll and a missed supper, though Yakov's gut alerted him to something considerably more daring.

At a quarter to six, the sky was already pitch black. Tense, dithering, and worn-out bodies treaded up and down the streets after a tedious day of labour. High street lamps illuminated the majestic, dizzying snowfall, but hardly anyone gazed upward to soak in its accentuated romantic charm. Yakov popped the collar of his wool trench coat, pulled on a pair of thin leather gloves stashed in his pant pocket, and fell a safe two dozen steps behind his target.

They were heading into Yakov's neighbourhood now, and knowing full well Sasha lived at the dorms, Yakov puzzled over the business he had here at this hour, and on a weekday, no less. The bustling centre behind them grew remote with every subsequent stride, the path narrowed, and the herd of pedestrians thinned. Yakov dropped back another dozen steps to elude detection.

Sasha's appearance was bedraggled; he was visibly unnerved. His body movements were unbalanced as he teetered from one end of the street to another like a drunkard. At one point, he leapt in front of an unsuspecting taxicab and was met with a creative parade of obscenities hurled at him by the driver.

Without so much as a flinch, the young man ignored the encounter and kept on. He turned onto Chkalov Street and made a sharp turn into an adjacent courtyard as if to cut through to his destination. Yakov kept watch; the area was all too familiar.

Sasha crossed the yard and headed for the entrance of an old, crumbling building. It projected a ghoulish illusion of slow sinkage under the hefty snowfall that steadily piled on the roof, the open balconies, and the windowsills. Arduously, he rubbed his palms together and jabbed the buzzer, waiting for the hatches to unlock. They clicked within seconds; he swung the door open and dove inside. Yakov was too far behind to see which apartment he buzzed, but he recalled the house to be Lady Ramazanova's place of residence. She was not taking pupils this late, he reasoned, and even if she were, Sasha was too old a student for her limited teaching capabilities. Admitting he could have been visiting someone else entirely, the coincidence was too great to dismiss. Yakov approached the door and gave it a tug; it was firmly locked. He dusted off a nearby bench and sat down in anticipation, hoping somebody would either go in or come out, providing him with a means to enter. Ten minutes elapsed when Yakov was ready to give it a rest and head home. It was too cold to sit about doing nothing, and he was late for supper as it was. Just as he stood up and turned on his heel, the door flew open, and a group of children raced outside with their toboggans. He rushed back and lodged his boot in the door before it locked.

Ascending the stairs on a light foot, Yakov tried his damnedest to remember correctly which floor Rama was on. While he walked Klara here many a time on reflex, she led the way, and his mind rarely engaged with the actual surroundings. He guessed it may have been the fourth floor and, having reached the landing, turned into a tight, yet far-reaching, dimly lit hallway. Faced with three possible apartments, the young man carefully pressed his ear against the first door, hoping to discern familiar voices. Having heard nothing, he moved farther down the hall on to the second apartment and, to great surprise, instantly detected Sasha's voice, heightened and churlish, but unmistakably his.

A female counterpart interrupted it shortly. She was also stern, albeit persuasive in calming her agitated guest. In their confrontation, Sasha griped of incriminating evidence, of being exposed, and of having to silence the traitors. Yakov had not a clue what it meant, or what kind of fraud a kid his age from a prestigious institution could get mixed up in. Maybe he was a gambler and owed money, or got in with the wrong crowd. How was that any of her business, and how could she – a petty, unsociable, kiddie piano instructor – help his cause?

Yakov settled to his knees as the acoustics became more pronounced. The walls turned out to be quite thin, and he contemplated how a full-time piano teacher got on in a house of such inferior construction, for the daily noise level and its ensuing echo must have rendered other tenants stark raving mad. The verbal tumult briefly subsided, followed by what Yakov perceived as a mounting physical scuffle. He readied himself to come to the aid of Lady Ramazanova had the struggle persisted, or if she called out for help. No such signal followed, however, and the ruckus that seemed violent just moments earlier now played like an amorous tussle. The bodies shifted to the back of the flat, and soon only muffled grunts and occasional moans broke the settling quiet. They were lovers.

Yakov chortled at the idea, thinking it a rather perverse arrangement, given their vast age difference. She was old enough to be Sasha's mother, and though he did not put a fetish of this nature past his eccentric peer, he was baffled by her apparent willingness to indulge him. Unsure he cared to eavesdrop any longer, he perched himself up and dusted off his trousers. His hand unconsciously weighed down on the lever handle, and with a gentle click, the door he was leaning on came ajar. Startled, he pulled it shut. Biting curiosity prevailed, and he lowered the handle again, this time sticking his head in the dark foyer. The bedroom must have been at the far end, for there were no lights anywhere as he tiptoed forward, terrified of knocking something over and making himself known.

A groan rang out so piercingly that Yakov squatted to the ground in shock. He was now on his hands and knees, crawling past the living room, and down the corridor. He heard another groan and then a thump. Finally, he made out a fine line of light under one of the doors in the far right corner. Yakov crept nearer, stopping short of the entryway. The door was closed. The old-fashioned keyhole, however, was generous and provided an unabridged view of the goings-on. He brought his eye to the opening and scanned the room, unable to believe what he saw.

This was no ordinary bedroom, but a space that bore resemblance to a medieval dungeon. The brick walls were bare, stripped of any paint, paper, or plaster. Dozens of oversized pillar candles illuminated the room housing a single metal cot in its centre, surrounded by dangling, thick chain contraptions that hung from the ceiling. Sasha lay on his back, naked, erect, and cuffed to the cot that, upon closer inspection, revealed itself as a stretching rack. Lady Ramazanova hovered above him, and with each escalating groan, turned the handle to increase the tension, until he spat out an inaudible phrase, a safe word, perhaps, and the torture came to a rapid stop.

Hesitant to observe more of the action, Yakov fell back and rested against the wall. Scratching his forehead, he recounted what he saw, still incapable and unwilling to accept it as truth. There was a flash of movement on the other side, and without warning, the door forcefully swung open. Yakov bolted back to the foyer, desperately trying to get on his feet, as her footsteps grew louder behind him. He was out of her apartment in seconds and galloped down the stairs, fearing he was made. Tumbling out of the building, he crossed the courtyard, dove into an alley, and emerged onto the main street. He ran home panting and gulping at the massive snowflakes that swirled around his face.

Yakov reasoned it was too dark for her to see him, and, just maybe, he was not made after all. Moreover, Ramazanova did not balk at her intruder; there were no screams and no fear, only mutual wonder. Perhaps she mistook him for a flustered customer who mixed up his appointment, but that theory had implications he was not prepared to take stock in. Did she moonlight as a madam, a dominatrix? Who was her clientele? The concept was too bizarre to believe. Not believing it was even more difficult.

When he got to his apartment complex and had a moment to breathe, Yakov realized one of his gloves was missing. To no avail, he patted his pockets, oblivious to whether he had dropped it in his street scramble, or worse, left it behind at her place.

To this day, the memory of the lost glove propelled him into a cold sweat because it marked the beginning of months spent wallowing in fixed doubt, a doubt that gradually matured into reality, and a reality that soon worked itself out as blackmail.

He did not pull Klara from her piano lessons, for a reasonable explanation was necessary, and regardless of how believable he made it, the timing was bound to raise suspicion. Whenever he dropped Klara off, he fretted over Ramazanova's penetrating stares and later speculated if he was exaggerating the whole affair. With that, February and March rolled on free of woe, and Yakov was starting to ease up about his quandary. What Ramazanova did on her own time was her business; as long as it did not interfere with and was of no danger to her pupils, he had no right to judge what he saw.

It was not until an evening in early April that the situation made itself known once again. Yakov was on duty at the library, packing up for the night with just a handful of folks scattered about the common area. He rang the bell, alerting the group to a five-minute grace before he shut off the lights. They stirred in their seats, cleared their tables, and readied to leave. Yakov was pulling on his blazer as the students walked past and nodded him farewell. He squatted below the front desk, unlocked the main console, flipped the switch, and marvelled at the smoothness with which the chandeliers dimmed one by one.

When he got back on his feet, his missing glove, not seen since the bitter January night, was resting before him on the coin platter. A bout of hysteria swept over him as he chased the remaining group down the corridor, with most having made it outside. He caught up with the last one, and swinging him round, materialized his worst fear. It was Sasha.

"Did you leave this at my desk just now?" he wheezed.

"It's yours, is it not?"

"Yes, how would you know that?"

"Same way you knew I am the one who dropped it off."

"It's been months!"

"I'm aware. We didn't need you 'til now."

Yakov was falling into a frenzy. "Need me? What for? And, who are we?"

"There's a job, we're a person short, and you're it."

"Now, just wait a minute, I've no idea what you think I saw or heard. It's none of my business, and I never told anyone, nor do I intend to."

"Of course, you don't. If you did, we wouldn't be having this conversation," he replied and started off. "I'll be in touch!"

From that point onward, Yakov could do little else but oblige. The "jobs," as there turned out to be more than one, were a vague term for something he dared not delve into. It could have been money laundering, drugs, or even prostitution. He kept his nose out of it and did strictly what was asked of him – dropping off small parcels at various locations around the city. He had no idea what was in them, or cared to ask, as it was unlikely he would be served with a sufficient, tangible answer. In the span of about a month, he engaged in a dozen drop-offs. Sasha routinely came by before the library's closing with an address and the load. Sometimes, he was direct with his transfers; other times, when the premises were extra crowded, he stashed the parcels around the building, leaving Yakov only a note.

At the start of May, he was scheduled to have another meeting with Sasha. Because it was the May Day holidays and the Bibliotheca was on lockdown, the duo arranged to meet after dark in a neighbouring courtyard. Yakov was intent on making this meeting their last, for his parents were getting wary of the sporadic, late-night telephone calls, knowing full well the friends their son did have would not allow themselves such impudence. He was ready to cut all ties, come of it what may. He pondered worst-case scenarios, sizing Sasha up to be no more than a young punk who thought himself something extra.

In truth, he, too, was a puppet like Yakov, maybe one of elevated standing in the hierarchy of puppets, but a puppet no less, and it was somebody else pulling the strings up top. That "somebody" may have been a first-class gangster or a third-rate wannabe thug. Regardless of his identity, this boss could reach out to Yakov directly if he so pleased, as Yakov was done taking orders from the rotten delinquent.

He remembered the day Klara came home from her play date with Dessa rather distraught, stating her friend left angry, and it was her fault for making it so. He was sympathetic, for his sister was a timid, fragile girl and did not indulge in many substantial friendships. When advising her to turn back and make amends, she retorted that Dessa had another date with Sasha and suddenly hushed up, realizing she had misspoken. He mulled over her words for hours, curious about Sasha's intentions with a girl so young. A horrendous thought sparked momentarily, and he squashed it with all of his might, for he dared not fathom that Sasha, even with his bouquet of deviant tendencies, could partake in utter moral obscenity.

Their meeting was scheduled for seven o'clock, and Yakov, burdened with anticipation, hurried forth across deserted streets. Upon entering the courtyard, he found himself decidedly alone. He waited for a staggering three quarters of an hour, kicking about in sand boxes and loafing on the swings. His peer never showed. He paced about the yard and resolved to take an extended stroll through the neighbourhood, thinking he could run into Sasha somewhere en route. The plan generated no payoff, and Yakov finally gave up and headed home. He reasoned the dilemma might have effectively solved itself, that his participation had run its course, or that a new dolt was badgered into this web of sordid affairs after also falling prey to the dastardly creatures. With any luck, Yakov would no longer be of service.

A day later, however, the telephone rang, and a hoarse voice on the other end inquired about a certain package that failed to arrive at its due destination. Yakov recounted his predicament, and though reluctant at first, the party took him at his word and hung up. Shortly, calls from exasperated characters searching for their loot were replaced by ill-tempered queries regarding Sasha's whereabouts.

Within a week, the harassment stopped altogether, and it was then that school officials alerted the staff to Sasha's untimely disappearance. Yakov did not express sentiment either way, for he feared becoming a person of interest in a mystery he had no share in. An investigation could effortlessly exploit his complacency with the shady dealings into something more weighty and sinister.

ঽ▲

The summer got off to a quiet start. Yakov again fell into a false sense of security, thinking the storm had blown over, and if no one had contacted him by then, they would not be contacting him at all. That was, until the detectives reached out with their photographs and reignited memories he duteously strove to suppress these past months. His parents were devastated, his sister humiliated, and he had no means to make any of it better.

These days, he kept afloat by putting one foot ahead of the other. Even though he was no longer active in the underground circles of fourberie and dreck, with Sasha still unaccounted for and presumably dead, there was little peace in his mind. Not a week prior, he had an off-colour encounter with Dessa in front of his flat. He came up on the girl out of the blue after quietly and, rather absentmindedly, ascending the stairs. She was facing away from him, her body pressed firmly against the door, consumed and unaware. He was reminded of her birthday and saw the jewellery casket Klara had wrapped so painstakingly earlier that morning.

When he called out to her, she went mad, the fear in her eyes so stark, he thought she had crossed paths with the devil. With her eyes bulging and lips stuttering, he could not explain why his presence rattled her so. As she scurried past, he noticed a beautiful porcelain figurine on the welcome mat. Turning to give it back to its rightful owner, he wondered if it, too, was a gift from Klara, and what trouble she went to in order to accommodate the exorbitant price tag. At the time, Dessa's odd behaviour was merely a cause for confusion. The more he thought about it, the surer he became that she mistook him for a threatening force with macabre intentions. He knew she was wrong about him, so what, or who, was the real threat behind her panic?

Yakov exited the archives and ambled through the library commons, tapping his fingers lightly on the dusty tabletops. Studies at the Braga Lyceum would resume shortly. Lamenting the evanescent nature of halcyon summertime, he dimmed the lights, threw on his knitted autumn cardigan, and headed home.

Chapter 14

In the late hours of a drafty September eve, Lady Rama's feet dangled from an industrial, ironclad lab stool, her arms bound behind her back by thick rope. Her single garment was a loose, ruffled nightgown, granting a frank, undisguised silhouette of the body when a light source was positioned just right. The rope was for show, as it was never secured tightly enough, and with one gentle pull, she could free herself instantly. Yet, it was precisely the illusion of being at Bud's mercy that so often aroused her.

Bud was in his late thirties and recently became employed at a French Consulate down the block. He and Lady Rama were acquainted when Bud stamped her visa papers six weeks earlier for her brief, school-sponsored summer vacation in Bordeaux. Shortly thereafter, he moved into an apartment building next door.

At their every meeting, Bud wildly gazed into her eyes to identify and assert her firm awareness of his domination. He relished in sensations brought on by his control, got off on her frequent squalls as he whipped her and convinced himself she was anxious to be taken mercilessly any which way at his will.

For Rama, Bud was starting to get predictable, and after weeks of illicit sessions, remained oblivious to the basic rule of domination: the submissive was always in control.

Whenever Bud finished with her, she threw on her robe and locked herself in the bathroom awaiting the definitive click of the front door to authenticate his departure. Every part of her body stung from the pain inflicted upon it by a man who was, in essence, a woman-beating scumbag masquerading as a fetishist, but one that managed to adequately fulfill her affinity for weekly doses of bodily affliction. Seeing herself physically bruised and emotionally weakened elevated her to a euphoric state of twisted comfort.

Rama's introduction to the business occurred about five years ago, when she attended a private bar after unrelenting persuasions from a former lover with whom she periodically kept contact, and who later revealed himself as the owner of the establishment. She had been teaching piano since her late twenties, and because of her hermetic lifestyle, was more than able to make ends meet with what little financial security the job provided. It was neither a comfortable employment nor a comfortable existence; and despite Rama's united love of music and children, she was not particularly successful with either. Her musical talent was average at best. Although technically sound, it was soulless in nature. Likewise, the failure to have her own children did not go unnoticed or unpunished in her circle. Occasional jabs at spinsterhood gradually turned into ridicule, and Rama was soon banished from the common social scene. Aging and alone, she yearned for noticeable change in her surroundings, for genuine risk in her encounters, and for variety in her sensations.

Her past lover's establishment functioned as an underground fetish club, the only one of its kind in the period before independence. Rama was never a naturally beautiful woman, but quickly found that the men at this bar could not care less about looks. Instead, they desired certain types of behaviour from their female counterparts. Outward appearances were of no matter on condition that one wholeheartedly obeyed the pursuit of either domination or submission. The members also discouraged each other from age bias, and in short order, Rama found herself returning to the spot on an almost weekly basis. It was not long before she transformed from a casual spectator to an active participant. There was high demand for women willing to engage in the taboo limitlessness of sexual power over their partners, so long as discretion reigned and brought no damage to the parties involved. Thriving in her newfound specialty, Rama led the ranks and was entrusted with a permanent position.

The pay was so high and her clientele so vast, that she endeavoured to forge a private service of her own. Determined, Rama converted a spare, windowless bedroom into a chamber of pleasures, ensuring her customers could have a go at any gadget they coveted, were it ropes, whips, branks, choke pears, chains, prods, shackles, tape, or specialty straps – she had an endless assortment. Catering to a very specific group of clients, her ex aided in constructing the space, adding on pillory stocks, the multipurpose stretching rack and, most notoriously, the Judas cradle, a device so unique and hardly attainable that even his establishment had yet to carry it. The accessories were smuggled in during night hours in large wooden crates to ward off the nuisance of neighbourly detection and subsequent, unwelcome curiosity.

In a good while, the exclusive circle of Rama's patrons widened when a string of regulars alerted her to trustworthy newcomers. Some dabbled once, others a handful of times, and then there were those she serviced for all of the five years she was active. For the past year, she upped the stakes, often allowing her patrons to stay the day and overnight. Those most aroused by the wait were privy to an extra-long stay. They were bound and gagged before her lessons, then left alone for hours, throbbing with pain and anticipation of rapture as Rama practised with pupils down the corridor. There were instances of close calls, with her subjects thrashing about in demand of recognition. The noise was largely undetectable to the children. To her trained ear, the men's wails grew louder, and she stroked the keys harder. Afterward, she punished them for their relentless intolerance, penetrating them with her gadgets as they writhed and howled in blissful agony. Her punishment was their most desirable pleasure.

A year ago, in the fall of '91, Rama got word from a regular of a new, interested customer. Said to be a young chap of twenty-two, Sasha Bandura was in his last year at the Conservatory and worked as a part-time ballet pianist with the Opera House's dance academy. When they first met, she instantly recognized him as the loner in the cafeteria, whom she had passed often on her way to the office and, for a while, was quite uncomfortable with the notion of participating in fetish games with someone so dangerously near her professional life. Anonymity was key, and all parties understood the delicate nature of their pastime. No one wanted to be outed, for this was no simple affair at the whorehouse, but something much more grotesque and misunderstood. To be publically labelled a deviant was a sure way to lose hard-earned social status, job positions, and family.

Rama and Sasha met every two weeks. After a handful of sessions, he confessed to her his other forbidden recreations. Perhaps, he estimated them, rather mistakenly, to be two of a kind and thought it appropriate to divulge the condemning information.

A mature tramp with that dungeon of hers, whom would she dare tell? Rama believed he drew satisfaction from unloading his secrets onto unsuspecting ears, conscious that she was in no position to judge or act upon his weaknesses.

Since then, she strove to occupy more and more of his time, thinking that, maybe, he could be hooked on a new, safer form of pleasure and, in consequence, be weaned off his revolting perversions. She was no longer an exclusive mistress, but a real-life paramour, venturing into a territory she had not explored for nearly a decade. Their affair was kept undisclosed to other patrons, for cavorting with customers outside of the set boundaries breached an already fragile and ever-shifting contract of power.

Rama soon discovered, however, that her efforts to turn him away from his deviancy were in vain. Having Sasha in the vicinity of her students was cause for greater arousal as he recognized both of his vices were now at arm's length. Although she doubted he was curable, to reject him now meant having considerably less oversight, and she could not reconcile with a thought of his involvement with the children she personally taught. The extensive and unsupervised access he had to the kids at the ballet academy was already catastrophic, and she debated if there was a manner in which one could anonymously persuade the faculty to let him go. Yet, the longer their affair lasted, the deeper into his abyss he dragged her, and Rama unceasingly cursed herself for so foolishly taking him on. She was forever trapped in his jaws, in a toxic cycle of boundless malevolence, one where he could callously act out her worst fears just to underscore and reinstate the control he had over their alliance. Little did she know, his local pursuits had long been realized.

He was gone now. The world was rid of him and his pestilence. She, too, was freed from his venomous grasp, and yet a day did not pass without a thought of a baneful evening in May that would infest her mind forevermore.

114

Returning to the city after the first weekend of May Day holidays, Lady Rama hoped to avoid an influx of all-too-insouciant locals who would shortly buzz about the streets like inebriated fruit flies, their bellies bloated with kabobs and homemade wine. She had a modest dacha on the outskirts of the city, making the forty-five minute trip by elektrichka every couple of weeks. And, despite the celebratory mood of her fellow citizens, this weekend was no different. The city, on the other hand, would be tranquil for days, allowing for extensive, leisurely strolls in the night with no interruptions and no fears for safety.

On these occasions, Rama packed a bag of mixed treats to have on hand for any furry friends she was to encounter along the way. The contents varied from old leftovers to cheap sausage franks she sometimes bargained for at the meat kiosk. Food scraps in tow, along with a bottle of sour milk, she meandered through the neighbourhood looking for strays to feed and to pet. Many were already introduced to her scent and approached with unabashed familiarity in hopes of a savoury handout. She never quite wanted a pet of her own, for her lifestyle could not readily accommodate another living creature. But, having a pack of tail waggers and purrers acknowledging her as one of their steady caretakers was plenty gratifying.

Excited at the prospect of engaging in another such night, Rama raided her refrigerator for treats, packed a small sack, threw on her shawl, and headed out. The sky was pitch black, its stars washed out by the street lamps; her wristwatch read close to midnight. It was the perfect time for the back alleyways to come alive, and Rama began to feel at home with the eerie sounds of the night. She passed through a neighbouring courtyard where, in one of the corners under a row of willow trees, stood a makeshift wooden trough with various scraps of meat and bone tossed about. A pack of dogs lived here and often scattered around other yards in search of food when their reserve ran empty. Another secluded pathway housed a kitten litter, and Rama gladly dispensed of her sour milk there.

Veering through abandoned parks and hidden passageways for nearly an hour, she ultimately found herself on the trottoir of Streletzkaya Street. It was cloaked in stiff quiet, and in the far darkness, Rama thought she saw a shadow stir. Spooked, she stopped dead in her tracks and waited for it to either stir again or prove to be a figment of her imagination. It was not so, and the shadow swiftly regressed into what looked like a path to a basement.

After contemplating a turnaround, Rama decided to bravely march on. Surely, she was not the only person left in the neighbourhood, and they, too, had every right to indulge in a solitary stroll of their own. As she approached the spot where she first laid eyes on the shadow, a door somewhere below her creaked open and the figure, now made out to be a man of some familiarity, emerged in a bit of a daze. He walked up the steps with some effort and faced her straight on. Droplets of sweat trickled from his forehead. Curiously overdressed for the typically warm nights of May, he wore a heavy wool suit and a pair of leather gloves, with his face partially obscured by a thick, knitted scarf.

"Hello, Rama," the man said.

That voice was unmistakable. She came closer and looked deep into his glazed eyes. It was he, after all.

"What are you doing here? I thought the family was off?"

"They are. And we have a bit of a situation on our hands."

"We? "

"Yes, you and I."

"I'm not sure what you mean."

"Well, about two minutes ago, it was my predicament and mine alone. Now that you've made me, you're either an accomplice or as good as dead."

116

"An accomplice to what?" she asked with a sharply drawn breath that vibrated through the balmy air.

His eyes shifted nervously to both ends of the street.

"Keep it down; we certainly aren't the only ones around."

"You're not making sense."

"Alright then, let me fill you in. I am in need of some help for a clean-up, and you'll have to do."

"What kind of clean-up? What are you on about?"

"The worst kind, I'm afraid. Go see for yourself," he turned and motioned her to the basement.

"I've no business going in there."

"And I can't let you leave, so go on."

She deliberated as he waited patiently for her conclusion. There was no way out of it. Being given a moment to think gave her a false sense of control over a decision that was already made for her. He generously extended his hand and led her into the basement. With teeth grinding and eyes half open, every muscle in Rama's body involuntarily convulsed at shrills of agitated vermin echoing throughout the structure.

"We seem to have a bit of a rat problem in these parts," he said sympathetically, observing she may not be of much use in her current state of paralysing distress.

"My building is the same."

Rama was unaware of what he was really after or, with their tumultuous history, if he sincerely planned to be rid of her had she protested his demands. The couple had not spoken in ages and were only cordial in public when so required. Now they were here alone, in a place that was, by all accounts, deserted.

Had she caused a ruckus, no one would hear. There were two guards at the Finnish Consulate farther along the road. Settling in their booth for the night, they rarely emerged to inquire about strange noises or to interfere in drunken disputes of the locals. They were locked away with their crossword puzzles, handheld radios and tellies, sipping on a warm bottle of cheap kvass while waiting for their shift to pass.

As he led her through a tight corridor, a stench of raw garbage nauseated her senses. When they reached the building's chute room, he paused and made way for her, lowering his head as a formal invite inside.

"Right through here," he said and threw her a grave look.
She proceeded inward, where a bright lantern balanced on the thick edge of a garbage trolley. Fighting for breath, she clenched her fists and took hold of her face, aiming to suppress the quiver in her lower lip. Sasha, her dear Sasha, was spread out on the concrete floor, his body stark naked and ashen.

"Oh God, is he—"

"Beyond all reasonable doubt, darling."

"And at your hands, I presume?"

"No, not this one. Though, I wouldn't be entirely opposed to the idea," he said, circling the body and pointing proudly to the throat. "You see? This here is an impressively deep and clean cut; something our kind would gladly take credit for." He stopped and smacked his lips in disappointment. "Sadly, not tonight."

She looked at him in disbelief. "You've gone mad. You're an animal!"

"I didn't do this, Rama. I'd have no problem telling you if I did, seeing as I already took the liberty to bring you here and incriminate myself."

"And now you've incriminated me as well."

"So it goes, old girl. I'd rather not dispose of this mess alone. I mean, I would have, until presented with an extra pair of beautiful hands. Think of yourself as my heaven-sent."

"What, no cronies you can call up? Get the gang together for one last hurrah? I'm sure they are better suited."

"There are no more cronies."

118

"No? You fell out?"

He was getting noticeably ruffled. "You're wasting my time. So here's an idea. We can't hide him only to be found by some drunkard a week later. We can't bury him only to have him dug up by a pack of strays. And we can't very well drown him, because those sly buggers always float up at the most inopportune of times."

"I won't be a part this."

"We're not taking a vote; it's going to get done."

"Or you'll off me, too?"

He let out a fiendish groan and leaped across the body toward her, tightening his left hand around her throat, and pulling on her hair with his right.

"Are you really trying to get a rise out me, old girl? Does it look like I'm in the mood for your infantine mind games? Or, do you honestly think that, if I have to go down for this shit, it will matter whether they get me on the count of one stiff or two? I don't give a damn about your juvenile feelings for this pathetic paedophile—"

Rama's eyes widened.

"Oh, was that a well-kept secret? Come on, woman, everyone knew you were fucking him off the clock, and all wondered if you got off on the idea that right before porking you he was feeling up little girls. Perhaps, you are as disgusting as he was. So, are you?"

His grip on her throat fastened; she was turning a deep, crimson red.

"No. No, I'm not. I didn't know, I swear to you."

"No need to swear to me. Not on your own miserable life, not on the life of your dead whore mother; save the pity party for another time. For the next hours, you aren't leaving my sight, and when it's over, we part ways. Whatever you think you'll have over me, I'll have over you as well, so either we take this to the grave or both of us burn. Is the dire picture of this a tad clearer for you now?"

"Yes."

"Oh, good. Then we can stop dicking around."

He let go of her at last, and she slid to the floor.

He was back to circling the corpse and stroking his forehead.

Rama pulled herself back up, composing her demeanour.

"Wh–what do you need me to do?"

He approached a duffel bag in the far corner that she failed to notice earlier and unzipped it, fishing out a large, clear kitchen tarp.

"Unfold it and place it there," he gestured, indifferently throwing it her way.

She did as asked, and he rolled the body over onto the tarp.

Sasha was on his stomach, which was pressing outward from the gases that had built up in his body. He no longer looked like himself, his form bloated, distorted, and unrecognizable. The boy's back was covered in bluish and purplish splotches from where the blood had pooled. He must have been dead for many hours, if not for days. It was now obvious this man did not kill Sasha, so who did? Why here, of all places and, most pressingly, why with such savagery? However technically impressive the kill may have been, it was carried out in a moment of sheer rage, or even passion; it was not a hired hit.

The man had tossed her some black garbage bags and was presently working something on a sharpening stone with his back turned to her.

"What is that?"

He spun around and showcased a massive, glistening meat cleaver, pressing his fingers playfully about its tip.

"Dear God, what is that for?"

He broke into a giddy laughter, amazed at her capacity for the silliest of questions.

120

She knew positively well what it was for, continuing to solicit him as a child would.

"Who did this? Who killed him?"

"Would it make a difference if I told you?"

"So, you know?"

"Of course, I know."

He moved over to the body and poked around the ankle of the right foot, taking a few exaggerated practice swings. Rama felt her innards churn and vomited on a nearby heap of garbage.

"Please, there are other ways, we can't do it like this. It's inhumane."

"Oh yes, my dear. Exactly like this. What does he care? He's dead! And the only way he is leaving this dump is in those bags, so, be a good girl and get them ready for me."

He knelt a bit lower, wielded the cleaver a tad higher, and hacked straight through the flesh and bone.

Piece by piece, Sasha's remains filled the opaque plastic bags. They were knotted off and stacked tenderly against the wall by Rama. Much to the man's disgust, she took her time with each bag, cradling it in her arms before setting it down.

"Maybe keep this one, old girl?" he scowled, tossing her Sasha's head when she turned around with another empty bag in hand, "You know, a memento of all the beautiful times you screwed each other in your amorous dungeon."

Rama squelched the onrushing nausea.

"No? Zero takers? Then be done with this sentimental shit. It churns my stomach."

He wiped down the cleaver, wrapped it in a newspaper, and placed the bundle back in his duffel bag.

"Fold the tarp," he ordered.

"And then what?"

"And then we're off."

"Off to where?"

The man popped out of the room with a whistle. "We're having a baby, my baby and me," he trailed off in song, clicking his heels and snapping his fingers while probing a dark nook of a service room across the corridor.

He reappeared, dragging behind him something large. "We're adding a limb to our family tree, we're pushing our carriage, how proud we will be!" he continued to croon.

"Now you've gone and done it," Rama carped as he stepped aside and theatrically showcased an old Silver Cross pram. "You think this won't attract attention?"

"No more than pulling bloated, stinking corpses in and out of trunks in plush Arabian rugs. A loved-up couple strolling with their baby carriage is inconspicuous even at this ungodly hour."

"You still could've used a car for transport."

"I could have, yes, except I don't know how to drive, remember? And until forty-five minutes ago, this was a lone job. So, have your laugh and start packing, whatever doesn't fit will go in my duffle."

Rama lined the pram with the smeared, folded tarp and placed the plastic bags inside. They were fifteen in total and four had to be shouldered by him. She popped the folding hood and secured the covering fabric apron. He turned off the lantern, and the pair headed out of the room.

The man led, surfacing first into the night to scout any unwanted company. When he gave the signal, she pushed the pram onto the short set of steps as he pulled on it from the front. Once on flat ground, they drew fresh air deep into their lungs.

"Where to?" she asked.

"The old meat packing plant, honey."

"It's been out of service for— oh, I see."

He beamed with childish glee and patted her bottom for her to push on.

122

Chapter 15

October's segue into November was a routinely dreadful stretch of time; the festive mood prefacing the winter holidays had yet to culminate, and the magic of autumn's changing foliage and fiery sunsets had slowly faded away, stranding the city's population in a grey, vacuous chasm of infirmity.

With a month and some left before the New Year, Dessa was determined to wrap up her intermittent address book excursions. She had neglected them indefinitely after the May debacle and could rarely be bothered to contemplate the unsolved mysteries that once fascinated her, nor did she take any real interest in anything or anyone else since then.

When she became convinced of Yakov as her arcane accomplice, her paranoia spiralled out of control. For weeks, she lost sleep, heard absent whispers, and saw fictitious shadows, realizing she was on the cusp of full-on madness, no differently, for that matter, than her unsung hero, Raskolnikov.

Having cast herself above the pangs of conscience, Dessa now experienced first-hand the psychosis, the all-encompassing illness one steadily, and often unwittingly, succumbed to in the wake of unprecedented murder. Her fear was not one of being haunted by the dead, nor the fear of being made anymore, but the strangeness of the unknown and the surreal, incessant state of sweeping dysphoria she had been drowning in for a good part of the year.

After much rumination, she finally took the last figurine as a peace offering rather than a perpetual taunt, a way for Yakov to showcase the totality and finality of their alliance, an alliance never to be spoken of and taken to the grave. No one, not even Klara, would ever come to know their secret.

It was with this mindset that Dessa hoped to rid herself of the nagging disquiet. The address book, however, remained a loose end. While the murder and the book had nothing in common, they were interwoven in a time the girl cared not to retain in her memory. She wanted to pay the last legible address a visit, and should it not yield any pertinent information, toss the address book and forget the day it ever came into her possession.

At first, she was set on going alone, later deciding to extend one final invite to Klara and Inna. Dessa was overcome with a perplexing case of profound nostalgia, as her feelings toward Inna were never congenial or accepting. Having spent little time in anyone's company as of late, the idea of a minor reunion, if only for a day, sounded plenty grand.

With the new school year, much had changed at the Opera House since the trio's admirable spring performance. No longer the queen bee among her younger peers, Inna was back with the corps de ballet for prima ballerinas in a higher year; Dessa graduated to a permanent coryphée and was fully content with what she regarded as an esteemed, yet stress-free position; and Klara was trapped somewhere in between, hopping from class to class and level to level on the weekly whims of Mistress Galina. The rare times they did interact were limited to exchanging brisk greetings in corridors, sluggish nods amid bathroom breaks, and frail smiles in the cafeteria during tea.

The plan was to meet once more after their respective rehearsals and continue on to the Golden Gates metro station as per usual. It got dark as early as four in the afternoon, and on a typical Sunday such as this, the metro's schedule was infrequent at best and proved entirely unreliable.

They would have to hurry, for the last address appeared to be on the far end of the Left Bank, the farthest they had ever travelled, and in spite of having time, weather, transportation, and distance stacked firmly against them, the trio chose to boldly forge ahead with their scheme. Transient thoughts of peril peppered Dessa's consciousness, and she debated if these inauspicious signs were alerting them to the foolishness of their quest, one that was best left untried, but hounding curiosity invariably trumped elementary reason. The youngsters pressed on.

Riding in the packed metro, Dessa bore an enduring sense of conclusiveness, a sort of termination of the trio's particular episode in the long-running series of life; a sense that how they were, right then, was the last time they would ever be. She did not quite understand the meaning behind it all, knowing only it was a fleeting moment never to be experienced the same way again. She no longer harboured any resentment or ill will toward either of the girls. In fact, there was a bit of wistfulness in the air about the three of them marching into the future; a future that, in all likelihood, no longer had them as friends or even in each other's immediate geographical vicinity.

Inna had turned fourteen and was transferred to a different class within the academy, confiding in them earlier that day that she would soon be attending a different school altogether. Her father was the recipient of a generous out through Hungary and was covertly readying his family for emigration. Inna seemed thrilled at the prospect of existing beyond the stifling borders, where fresh starts guaranteed people a new lease on life.

Dessa repeatedly questioned if she, too, would one day be granted an opportunity to leave all she held dear and venture into the great unknown. It could be better, a lot better; it could be worse, or in the most probable and mundane scenario, it could be more of the same.

When they arrived at the last stop, there was still a half hour's worth of ground to cover by foot. The girls fastened their scarves, pulled down their rabbit shapkas, and trekked through ankle-deep sludge on the lopsided trottoirs. Nothing this side of the river ever garnered much praise; the insides and outsides of structures were gnarly, their upkeep inadequate if not altogether forsaken.

Meanwhile, the inhabitants simmered in a heightened grade of destitution, their blanched semblances rarely shifting anywhere beyond the learned, limited spectrum of moroseness.

"You still think those missing girls and the address book are connected?" inquired Inna after a seemingly eternal silence.

"I guess, I don't really know anymore," Dessa shrugged.

"You sounded so certain back then."

"A lot of time has passed. Even if they were connected, I'm not sure what good that knowledge will do us now."

"I bet all of them are still missing. You know, most of the time, they never find any of the disappeared folk."

"Wouldn't you think most of them are dead, then?" chimed in Klara at last.

"I'd presume so," said Inna. "I mean, where else would they be, if not dead?"

"Tortured, perhaps," Dessa speculated, "maybe even forced into prostitution or hooked on heroin, cocaine—"

Inna ruptured into a deafening snicker.

"Been watching a bit of Traffik, have you? I must say, Daddy's been very strict with me about it, even though I'm older. That's a great theory you've got going, just like the movies!"

126

"Yeah– sure, like the movies–" said Dessa, not knowing what was more terrifying, to learn those girls were already dead, never to be found, or that they were alive and suffering at that very moment, strung up, drugged out, waiting like cattle to be auctioned off to the highest bidder for an extra dose of abuse.

She was struck with a memory of the ghostly mother and reflected on the agony she was destined to stew in for the rest of her life. The pain her missing daughter may have been in, and, quite possibly, was still in, persuaded Dessa to conclude that both women were better off dead.

"I don't think this is going to bring closure in spite of what we may find today," she continued. "I just wanted to exhaust the locations, to have ourselves a sort of wrapping up, if you will. Though, I'd argue we've made for pretty insufficient detectives so far."

"It could be because there's nothing to solve."

"Or, it could be that possessing any real knowledge on this matter requires persistence and a network of sources we simply have no access to."

"Spoken like a true telly private eye!" Inna smirked.

"She's the next Zheglov," giggled Klara.

"And we're looking for our own Black Cat gang!"

"With evil Foxes and Hunchbacks abound!"

On any other day, Dessa would be fuming at her cohorts' waggishness, thirsting to have left the cackling nitwits behind. Right then, she thought of nothing better than falling back and taking in their jeu d'esprit.

The trio was now upon Tumanovskaya Lane, an eerie title for the murky, phantasmal surroundings coating the living quarters about the block. The gliding fog gave a haunting illusion of shifting structures, sparking a fear that, at any moment, the ground could shift beneath their feet, give way, and swallow them whole.

The scene reminded Dessa of an incident she witnessed at a tender age of four, maybe five, when the basement of their apartment complex caught fire. She stood on the balcony of their fifth floor flat looking down at the plumes of smoke she took for a heavy fog nimbly frothing from the ground itself in order to envelop and devour the building. When Mother snatched her up and locked the patio doors, she was confident they were sinking into the ground, recalling no smell of smoke or signs of flames, just an ominous, chalky fog rising, tormenting. To stand knee-deep in it now felt even more terrifying.

"Are you coming?" said someone in the distance.

Dessa found herself alone, the fog so thick she could no longer make out the others ahead. She followed their chatter, or what she believed to be their chatter, as the voices grew isolated with each panic-stricken step. Klara was in possession of the address book, and Dessa could not make out the numbers of the buildings around her. A warm surge rushed through her limbs, an all-too-familiar feeling she had not experienced since the episode at Lady Rama's over a year ago. She fought within herself, trying to convince her uncooperative body this was not the time, yet her knees weakened, and she was tempted to give into the darkness. Shutting her eyes, she felt a cold hand yank at her wrist and pull her forward. It was Klara.

"We located the flat. Have you no interest to go in?"

"I was feeling somewhat lightheaded."

"Should we turn round?"

"No, no. Let's do it, where's Inna?"

"She went forth."

"Alone?"

"It's just another complex, I'm afraid. Same as the others. These trips have proven fruitless."

"Still better than moping about at home, I suppose."

128

Klara led them to an entrance. The gate was ajar, and the duo slipped inside, fussing up the staircase where Inna waited unassumingly, stroking the blonde locks flowing freely from under her shapka.

"Second floor," she said, nodding upward. "We should ring the doorbell this time."

"And say what, exactly?" protested Klara.

"If a man answers, we pretend to have the wrong flat, apologize, and head out. If it's a woman, we ask whether or not she has a daughter."

"And then what?"

"We can play it by ear, no?"

"That doesn't sound like much of a plan."

"Well, we haven't come all this way to double-check numbers on a door, have we?"

"I reckon not. In that case, you take the lead," Dessa said, symbolically handing over the reins. She was taken aback by Inna's sudden brazenness, a trait she also possessed and admired in others, but one she never suspected to surface in a Goody Two-shoes like Inna. Perhaps, Mister Dvorkin's lifelong shenanigans had finally left their mark on his humorously pious daughter.

The girls shuffled up the steps, coming to face a ragged front door with its leather lining frayed and cheap, its plastic stencils glued haphazardly off-centre to read "59." The welcome mat was a single piece of crumpled, maroon cloth; the ringer's button was jammed and rough to the touch.

Inna swallowed hard and squashed it with all available might, only to make out a faint, uneven chinking across the wall.

"Nobody home," said Klara without conviction. "I'll ring again." Reaching for the bell, she was intercepted by Dessa.

"Don't, it's better if we go."

"What's with you? Nothing's going to happen."

"I'd rather go," maintained Dessa.

Before the girls could turn back, a patter on the other side grew nearer. There was movement at the peephole, followed by a reluctant, guarded turning of a key. The handle bent, and the door cracked open a notch. A pair of distrustful, sunken eyes ogled them through the minuscule slot.

"What business have you here?" hacked a deep, female voice.

"We are sorry to bother you like this, Madam," started Inna. "We're looking for someone and were wondering if you happened to have a daughter."

"Daughter?"

"Yes, one that's gone missing, perhaps?"

"Who are you?" mouthed the woman, fidgeting audibly, eyes widening. "Who sent you?"

"No one sent us, Madam."

"You must go quickly," she hissed. "They've been watching us, and now they are watching you, too."

"Who is? There's no one here but us."

The slot widened, and Dessa glimpsed a figure in the background, a girl of their age.

"Go now," reiterated the woman.

"Oh, Madam! Please, we mean you no harm!" pleaded Inna. "We have no more than a couple of questions."

The door flung shut; the key twisted violently; footsteps retreated.

"We'd better heed her warning," Dessa pronounced, shaken by their exchange.

"Don't tell me you're scared. She's a paranoid old bat."

"No, I don't think so."

"I agree, we should scram," spoke up Klara.

Without waiting for Inna's consent, Dessa descended the stairs and exited the complex. The others joined her momentarily, and the trio started on their tedious trek back.

Darkness fell faster than usual, amplifying the malign ambience that had taken hold. Dessa was spooked to her very core. She heard brisk steps behind them and spun around, coming face to face with the young girl from the apartment above. She bore a striking resemblance to Inna, standing just as tall with the same luscious strands of blonde hair.

"You said you were looking for my sister?"

"We didn't mean to upset anyone, we're sorry," professed Inna, stepping closer.

"No one has looked for her in years, not now, not when she first went missing. Our pleas, flyers, promises of rewards... No one bothered to search, even then."

"What about the police?"

"Especially not the police."

"Tell us your name," Dessa urged.

The girl shook her head, biting her lips, her eyes shifting about the street. "How did you get here?" she asked.

"By metro, then we walked. We're from the Right Bank," enthused Klara.

"I mean, how did you find us?"

"We came across an address book," Inna said.

"Shut up, Inna," Dessa scathed, "not another word."

"What does it matter? It's another dead end."

Dessa turned to the stranger. "If you know more than your mother let on, then speak up. Otherwise, there was no reason to follow us."

"I was curious."

"So are we."

The girl scanned the area and, convinced of their anonymity, leaned into the trio.

"She was eighteen when they took her. They take younger ones, too, even prefer them sometimes, but she didn't look her age. If you see them, they'll take you, too."

131

"Why were you spared, then?" noted Dessa.

"I never said I saw them."

"I know you did. I see it in your eyes, the fear."

"We keep quiet, mind our own business, don't show our faces. They come to remind us every now and then."

"So, you live in a self-imposed prison?"

"They show mercy, if you keep quiet."

"And just who are 'they'?" Inna burst out impatiently.

Startled, the girl began to backtrack toward her complex.

"Wait, please don't go," appealed Dessa. "Have you the slightest idea if your sister is alive at present? If you can explain any of it, just answer that."

The girl teetered in the slush, steepling her fingers.

"Yes, though she was dead the moment they took her."

A car started somewhere in their radius, and the girl, without any added clarification, turned on her heel and hurried home. Overwhelmed by the flow of sensitive information, the trio kept motionless.

"And now we know everything," declared Inna triumphantly.

Dessa was exasperated. "Everything and nothing, seeing as we are now left with even more questions we can't answer."

"Sounded pretty clear to me. Dare I say, your earlier telly-inspired musings sound spot on, bravo!"

"Oh, come off it."

The girls started again, veering into a poorly lit alley. Dessa picked up her pace, wanting to traverse the darkness with maximum speed. Klara put a skip in her step, doing her best to keep up, while Inna drew back, afraid that adopting a rapid stride would needlessly soil her dainty, periwinkle overcoat.

A car steered into the alley, its bright headlights alerting everyone to a new, foreign presence. Dessa perceived the car's approach, anticipating it to pass them at any moment. She heard a piercing screech of tires instead. Doors clicked open; unknown bodies tramped into the slush. At last, she stopped and twisted round. The alley was too dark, the beaming headlights immobilizing. She slogged back, taking hold of Klara, who was equally aghast at what unfolded in front of them.

"Inna!" they screamed, met with a series of muffled yelps.

She was struggling with two towering shadows, kicking incapably at the mud beneath her feet. Getting her wits about her, Dessa charged at the culprits, who were now moving toward their car with Inna in tow. Klara shouted for help with tears cascading along her flushed cheeks. As Dessa advanced, she was met with a jarring blow to the face. Losing her balance, she toppled to the ground, detecting a hint of metal in her mouth. A hard swallow tasted as if a handful of kopeks got lodged in her throat. One of the shadows slouched above her, taking off his thick leather gloves.

"Leave her," ordered a stern, raspy voice from the car.

The warm surge was taking hold again, and before Dessa gave way, she recognized something on the shadow's wrist, an obscure mark previously seen in that exact spot on somebody else. Not a mark, she thought, a tattoo.

"Uncle?" she spoke softly, her vision fading to black.

ê

Dessa awoke to arguing voices in the corridor outside of her room. One of the voices, familiarly high-pitched and loquacious, was undeniably Mother's; the baritone, lyrical speech was Shurik's; and a third voice, laconic, dry, and unremarkable, remained a mystery.

Lamps were dimmed, with curtains pulled halfway over her windows. The clock read a quarter past ten. Her jaw ached; an attempt to grind her teeth yielded terrible, pulsating pain; a rotten, metallic taste lingered. The hallway chatter amplified, the doorknob twisted, and the parties entered. The unidentifiable voice was that of Dr Izmailova, a feisty, middle-aged, Georgian woman and local paediatrician, the only one willing to make house calls at this hour of night. Shurik reached her bedside first, pulled near a chair, and rolled up his sleeves.

"You lost a couple of teeth there, darling. Good thing they were due to come out anyway," he said, raising his grey, caterpillar eyebrows.

She flexed her tongue, feeling for the emptiness; a lower central incisor and an upper right premolar were missing.

"Where are they?"

"You must've spit them out or swallowed them, dear."

"I can't remember."

"You don't have to, just rest."

"Come on, Papa," Mother insisted.

"Not now. Let her be."

Dr Izmailova took a seat on the bed and opened her Gladstone bag. Fishing out a stethoscope, she lifted Dessa's pyjama blouse and slipped the chest piece under. The girl squirmed. The poking and prodding lasted mere minutes, and Izmailova was heading back into the corridor.

"I want to know what you were doing out there," said Mother, "and until I hear a satisfying truth, you're punished."

"Enough with that," Shurik countered.

"No, Papa, she must be held accountable."

"Where is Klara?" asked Dessa, sitting up suddenly in her bed. She summoned to mind her friend's cries and the shadowed men who abducted Inna; had they snatched poor Klara as well?

"You are not to see that Jewess again," said Mother with a childish stomp. "I forbid it!"

"I didn't ask to see her, Mother, I asked where she was. I'd like to know if she's alright, that is all."

"Cheeky monkey!"

"I'd like to rest now, if you don't mind." Dessa glanced at the door, hoping Mother would see herself out promptly. She dared not waste precious time humouring the grownups; there were things to be done and questions to be answered. Finding Klara was imperative.

"Alright, darling, as you wish. We'll touch base come morning. I hope you'll have much to tell us," said Shurik.

He gave her palms a gentle squeeze and motioned Mother into the hallway. As soon as the door shut, Dessa sprinted out of bed and rushed to the windowsill. Gusts of sleet crusted the pane as she unlocked it; extending her hand out into the thrashing downpour, she felt for an old soup can beneath the cornice. Although the girls had not partaken in these types of exchanges for some time, the impending house arrest left Dessa no choice. This was a trusted, furtive method of communication, secure from adult interception and prying eyes; she only hoped Klara would realise it soon enough in order for them to proceed.

At her secretary, she jotted down a brief note.

"Are you safe? How did I get home?
Punished indefinitely, no contact."

She folded the scrap of paper, sealed it in a small plastic bag, and placed the contents inside the soup can. She let it hang and pulled on the thin, looped clothing line, sending her message laterally and downward to the third floor. The window there was not for an apartment, but an alternate stairwell where Klara would have to go. She could have been punished herself, rendering any attempts at communication fruitless. Dessa was determined to try. The rope stalled; her message had reached its destination. There was nothing left to do but wait.

Chapter 16

The days following Inna's abduction glided by in dreamlike slow motion. Dessa was made to stay home, suspending her dance rehearsals and academic duties for upward of two whole weeks. The family's tutors were on call, and she kept shape with an old ballet barre in the corridor she had long outgrown, as it retained its basic functionality and made do in unforeseen, tense circumstances such as these.

Three days in, there was no word from Klara. It was becoming more likely that she, too, faced similar consequences. It could have been any number of things, really; the soup can was flimsy, and with unrelenting strong winds and downpours, may have easily tipped over, sending Dessa's message straight for the barren flowerbeds below; or perhaps Klara simply did not recall their makeshift wire system and schemed of no other way to make contact. Dessa ruled out the possibility of a double abduction, reasoning if that were the case, Mother and Shurik would not be so unusually cruel as to keep her thoroughly uninformed. Besides, a double kidnapping ensured inevitable police involvement, and no one had called or went snooping round since she came to. Sorting through these sentiments, she had to assume Klara was safe and home after all. The wait continued.

It was on the sixth day, late in the afternoon, when gloom had already blanketed the skies, that Dessa heard a solid clink outside her window. The soup can had made its way back and supplied a new message. She tore anxiously through the plastic and unfolded two pages worth of writing. Dessa dropped to the floor right where she stood and began to read.

My dearest friend,

There is much to tell you, where do I start? With answering your initial questions, I suppose. Yes, I am safe, as safe as one can be in these strange and uncertain conditions. The black Volga that captured Inna left you on the side of the road, unconscious and bleeding. It sped right past me, though I was confident it was going to be my end as well. I dragged you to the sidewalk and ran back to the apartment we'd just visited. No matter how long and loud I pleaded for assistance or, at the very least, the use of a telephone, the building had turned into a ghost house. When I came back out to tend to you myself as best I could, a large, unmarked van was driving away from where I'd left you. It was unlike any ambulance I ever saw, not an official one. I figured they weren't the enemy, as the previous brutes could have taken you, if they so pleased. It occurred to me I was still in possession of the address book, having forgotten to give it back to you in the commotion.

I took the metro home, and confided in Yakov the sordid details of the day. There was nobody to turn to, no one else I could think of to trust. This came as a real blow to him after all that transpired earlier this year. He knew more than he let on, I think, judging by the grave way he paced back and forth about the flat. He said he would have to walk me everywhere from now on "until the dust settled" and confiscated the address book at once. Forgive me, for I doubt there is a chance of getting it back now. What he did with it, I've no idea, and part of me is relieved that the bundle of terror is no longer in our hands. I can't say what will happen or when we'll see each other next, though I do hold faith our nightmare will not persist forever.

Lastly, I overheard Yakov on the telephone (the party on the other end stands unknown). He spoke of a trade, an oath of protection, an insurance from "higher ups" that no more harm comes to any of us and insisted on summoning "Leo" immediately. On any other day, I'd chock it up to mere coincidence, but my current state of angst and desperation leads me to believe it could very well be your Uncle Leo. What would be his involvement with any of this?

It is with great difficulty that I am able to sneak out, so if you do write again, allow a couple of days for reply. Please, accept my sincere apologies for failing to write sooner; I had nearly forgotten our little secret.

Do not despair, for even the most unyielding of storms will reach a calm.

–Klara

Dessa reread the letter several times, concluding that Klara's retelling served to raise more unanswerable questions. Everyone knew more than they let on; everyone had unnamed contacts, made late-night calls, and possessed information invaluable to someone else. Some drove black Volgas through deserted alleyways snatching up unsuspecting persons; others set out on foot, lurking in stairwells, basements, and courtyards. It had the trappings of the macabre, as if they were stuck in a cinematic hallucination with no suitable ending and not a glimmer of hope on the horizon. Her choice to cross the boundaries of human decency, to conceal it, and then revel in it without the slightest hint of remorse had set off a cataclysmic chain of events, events she understood to have everything and nothing to do with each other.

Dessa suspected her dark, though unsubstantiated, reveries about Uncle Leo's true occupation had ultimately rang true. It was only a matter of time, and the time to call upon him was now. She knew for a fact the man who knelt over her that night was not Uncle, yet their tattoos were identical. They were markings of power, emblems of exclusivity and elusiveness, be it a class, or an organization that could possibly absolve her of any wrongdoing and, maybe, bring Inna back.

Even so, the bouts of optimism were fleeting; something told her Klara's perception of the goings-on was askew. The storm had not passed; the calm they were entering was the calm before the storm, and the worst was yet to come.

Dessa hid the letter under a stack of notepads in her desk drawer and went to inquire from Mother about placing a call.

ࠫ

Getting hold of Uncle Leo proved to be no small feat. Mother was hovering too close, intrigued by the urgency with which her daughter sprang into action in order to locate him. She was not especially friendly with her brother; he was the heir apparent to a potential fortune, not in the mundane monetary sense, rather in a timeless aura of respectability evoked by the Faustov name alone. A name that had served him well, but one he often resented and did not much care for, deliberately failing to credit it with any successful ventures or opportunities that would not have been granted otherwise. He did, however, take pleasure in the rare company of his niece, and Mother speculated he could uncover some coherent, satisfactory truth behind the happenings on the Left Bank that Dessa refused to acknowledge altogether, much less articulate on. After exhausting a myriad of friends and acquaintances, some of whom had unexpectedly turned foes, Dessa located Leo on the far outskirts of the city, and was promised a bedtime visit later that night, if so permissible by Mother.

At a quarter to eleven the doorbell rang. Dessa lounged in bed, tuning into the brief, cordial greetings in the foyer as heavy footsteps advanced in the direction of her room. A confident knock on the door, without a wait for confirmation, was followed by Leo's businesslike entrance. As per usual, he was impeccably dressed, sporting his signature Chesterfield lined with a beige opera scarf; and though Dessa saw him year round, she struggled to conjure up an image of him ever wearing anything else. He peeked back into the corridor, assuring Mother was out of reach, and shut the door tightly.

"Good evening, sport," he said, placing his charcoal suede gloves on her vanity and giving the room a quick scan. "Or is it? A good evening, I mean." He threw Dessa a knowing wink.

"Oh, Uncle!"

She chucked the covers and ran to him, burying her slender body in the folds of his overcoat.

"There, there, you've got to be a good girl and stay strong. We'll sort this out in no time."

"Much has happened," she sobbed.

"So I am told."

He took a seat in Dessa's spacious fauteuil and motioned her to join him on his lap.

"I think you'd better start this one from the beginning."

Dessa fidgeted with her fingers, comfortably drowning in Uncle Leo's masculine amplitude, uneasy of the judgement he was bound to pass. She used to despise the company he kept and the frivolities he shamelessly endorsed, and yet, to fail in his eyes now seemed unthinkable and irreversible.

140

"There were three of us that night, Klara, Inna and my–"

"The real beginning, sport."

"How do you mean?"

His gaze was steady, his silence patient, but stiff.

"Alright," she started over, "it must've been a year and a half ago that Klara and I stumbled upon a lost address book."

Uncle Leo reached into the breast pocket of his dinner jacket.

"Like this one?" he asked, holding up the leather notepad Klara claimed to have surrendered to Yakov.

"Where did you–?"

"Keep going."

"We found it in a flower bed by the French Consulate."

"Scatterbrain. Of course!" he mumbled.

"We asked around, Uncle, I swear! No one laid claim to it, so we thought it was safe to keep."

"And what have you been taught about taking things that don't belong to you?"

"Those art books didn't belong to you, either," she snarled, astonished at his audacity and urgently apologetic.

Uncle Leo's lips stretched in a mischievous smile. "Saucy bugger."

"I am sorry, Uncle, we just wanted an adventure."

"And an adventure you most certainly got."

"We were very careful, visiting the addresses from time to time. They yielded no clues. That is, until I spotted a message board of missing persons, whose addresses matched a few from the address book. It was all very strange, and I couldn't help but suspect foul play."

"Smart girl. Why rekindle it now?"

"We were left with one location, and something always came up. It was just recently that we had time to get together again, reckoning we'd toss the address book after this last visit."

"I see."

"It all went so terribly wrong. Inna was taken, and I got hurt. You can bring her back, you have that power."

"How do you figure?"

"The man who hit me had your tattoos."

Uncle Leo bit his lips, his gaze turned pressing. "Isn't that a curious coincidence?"

"Those men had every chance to take me. They didn't, and I am certain you are to thank for it. I won't rat you out, Uncle, cross my heart. You've got to help."

He sank deeper into the fauteuil.

"Even if I did have any weight in the matter, you've never cared for Inna before, why the sudden solidarity?"

"Whatever they thought we knew, none of us were going to make trouble. She's done nothing wrong, and I feel responsible."

"Quite the wavering moral compass you've got there, kiddo." A hint of deviancy flickered in his eyes.

"Are you with the Mafia?" Dessa asked at last, and Uncle Leo exploded with laughter.

"No, sport. Nothing so glamorous, I'm afraid."

"And your tattoos?"

"What of them?"

"They've got to mean more than what you claim. Please, she doesn't deserve any of this, and her family must be worried senseless. I can't imagine what they'll do to her."

"Isn't that what policemen and detectives are for?"

"They are probably in on it and will do nothing!"

"Is that so, my little firecracker? This sounds like very serious business and may require considerable sacrifice."

"Whatever it takes, Uncle, we have to right this."

"I doubt you realize just how much is at stake."

"I'd give everything I have to bring her back safely, honest!"

"That's quite a liberal offer, parting with your most prized possessions for the safety of another."

142

"In a heartbeat! Does that mean you can help us?"

"I'll tend to the situation. I make no promises."

She cheered, wrapping her arms around his broad shoulders as he raised himself from the fauteuil and reached for his gloves. She gave him a kiss on the cheek and raced to her secretary; a joyous letter to Klara was in order.

"Not a word of our exchange is to be uttered to Mother or Grandpapa, understood?"

"Yes, sir."

Leo reached for the doorknob, clutching it idly. "And Dessa?" he said quietly, "This is the second time in a very short time. I must say you're draining my generosity with lightning speed."

She dropped her pen, reluctantly turning toward him. Time stood still. Something, a kind of muted comprehension, passed between them. He turned the knob and walked himself out. She thought she saw him flash her a crooked smile, yet, upon closer observation, maybe, it was not a smile at all.

Chapter 17

Previously, on the Sunday evening of 3rd May 1992, Leonid trotted along Georgievsky Lane, a scenic, discreet path running perpendicular to Streletzkaya Street where he periodically resided. He was scheduled to meet business partners in the area, but business was dwindling, the numbers were low with profits marginal at best, and he was in no hurry to make it. These impromptu endeavours to rally the troops were starting to annoy him. Everyone had use of a telephone, rendering the need to touch base in person completely unnecessary. Having no desire to needlessly flash his mug more than he had to or to spend an evening looking at others', he contemplated giving the business up for good.

A noble thought it was, one that existed solely in the folds of his imagination, creeping in during prolonged solitary strolls, lonesome nights in front of the telly, or drunken heart-to-hearts with drifters such as himself. In truth, once you were in it, there was no time off, no retirement with old age, and no getting out, not even in death.

His father's ideals never quite suited him. He didn't believe in placing high value on material things, for they, too, like money, were meant to be passing and fluid. He pontificated about their ancestors as fools who starved to death whilst sitting on priceless chairs they were too haughty to sell for a bread loaf, calling the preservation of physical history a useless pastime, namely when you ended up below ground doing it.

Unfortunately, Leo's adopted circle of racketeers soon bred matching resentment. None of the petty vandals, hustlers, and traffickers of whatever was currently in demand were on par with the greats they so crudely imitated. They were feared, dangerous people, but not in the romantic fashion Leo aspired. There was something to be said for handling affairs with prestige and finesse, even in the lowliest rings of the underworld.

The meeting place was an abandoned construction site, a housing complex scheduled to undergo major overhaul seven years ago that had since stalled indeterminately. An abundance of deserted renovation projects peppered the city's skyline, indiscriminate of the areas' social and historic hierarchies in which they stood. Leo was convinced these structures of rubble were directly responsible for the spike in second-string crime rings by affording them unlimited spaces of anonymity to foster unfettered corruption. Had promises of residential expansion and grandeur been promptly married with deed, the rise of bottom feeders would not be as rampant, or so he assured himself.

Upon reaching his destination, Leo lit a smoke and made his way to the fourth floor where the rest of the gang proceeded to argue loudly. The virtual emptiness of the city turned otherwise leery scoundrels into boisterous ninnies, and Leo felt asinine by association. There were six in total, each with a set of responsibilities to keep the money wheel turning. Someone had dropped the ball, and the bosses upstairs were taking names. Nobody knew how high the chain of command went, for every crime ring functioned as a branch of another and then another, making it nearly impossible to trace anyone's origins.

The current dilemma required a snappy fix, so the group looked to their resident rich boy for extra cash before they were all ordered to hang, and while Leo had no scruples about pawning the family's fortunes, he did take offense to the contemptible, wide-ranging pool of degeneracy his episodic sponsorships helped sustain. Had the boys put their brains together, they could have freed themselves from the iron grip of the system, creating a new criminal elite unmarred by the cheapness of candy men, pimps, and paedophiles. Instead, these idiots fought like rabid dogs over every last scrap, and Leo often questioned how the glamorous world of outlaws had turned out to be so excruciatingly ordinary.

The gang gathered round, brainstorming how much everyone could chip in to temporarily adjust the deficit. Leo remained on the sidelines, unwilling to engage in the indignity of their haggle. Resting on a concrete block near the window openings, he looked out onto the languidly dimming horizon, able to spot the treetops of his own courtyard. There was talk of auxiliary cash reserves stockpiled about the city by the bosses themselves in an event of a crisis, and the crew unanimously concurred their existing predicament called for desperate measures. Paying their debt with the mob's own money was an ingenious scheme, and if found out, its repercussions ensured certain death. The task, had they chosen to pursue it, was not to be taken lightly, and Leo was doubtful his so-called partners were intellectually capable of seeing it through.

Rumours suggested one such reservoir was buried in this neighbourhood, containing a mix of rubles, German marks, Swiss francs, and half a dozen gold bullion bars. Latest reports placed the loot in Saint Sophia's nunnery, which was shut down and vacated for repairs. This coincidence could not have been timelier, posing them with unrestricted access to the unmanned property. A draw for a stakeout ensued, which Leo cut short.

"I'll go," he volunteered, eager to be left in peace.

To his surprise, no one challenged, probably thinking that had anything gone wrong, he could bite the dust on his own without implicating the rest of the pack. Cold, calculating bastards they were, but every last man was expendable, and Leo was not about to bask in special treatment. The crew shook on it, and one by one, ditched the hideout.

He stretched on the pleasantly cool concrete and lit his last cigarette. There were hours to waste before embarking on the surveillance, and he planned on spending them right there, immobile and dazed. His senses fell prey to the intoxicating, fused aromas of lilacs and blooming acacia trees, their potency ever-shifting with each gentle breeze. He fantasized about how far he could get with the stash, had he found it, if it were feasible to run with it and keep on running. True liberty was out there, outside of these walls, this neighbourhood, the city, beyond any geographical borders; it was calling, tempting newcomers to pursue it, embrace it, and never look back. An arduous quest this freedom was, for whenever Leo sensed he was closing in, it repeatedly evaded him, drifting provocatively out of range.

The high-rise clock in the Independence Square struck nine, reverberating by way of vacant avenues of the sleepy downtown. Leo rose from his languor, prepared to leave, yet unable to move. With his head stooped and feet heavy, he searched for the will to escort himself out into the night. Staggering in and out of collapsing passages, he withdrew from the construction maze and headed for the nunnery.

The cathedral's estate had numerous staff entrances, all secured, though unproblematic for an average lock picker. Leo was above average and did not mind the hustle, as the towering stone fence enclosing the grounds was too high to climb. He chose a gate positioned directly behind the Monastic Inn to avoid any superfluous movement about the gardens on the odd chance the bell tower monk had left his post. The two-bit lock yielded in a flash. He was in.

Leo surveyed the cloister, gliding through the arcades, his strides veiled by morphing shadows. He gained access to the inn via its kitchen, minding the torn-up flooring yet to be re-tiled and moved into the refectory, tiptoeing about the creaking parquet. Checking off the rooms, he explored irregularities within the structure, turning out every hollow, nook and cranny. His hunt was coming up short; the nunnery had naught to offer. The dormitory was his last stop, and he rested on a low-set, shaky cot, slumping into the uneven straw mattress. With his smoke pack depleted, Leo sucked on a stalk of wheat instead, hoisting it up to his mouth on the beat and pursing his lips as he exhaled. It occurred to him this layout ought to accommodate a granary or a cellar, his last resort before having a go at the gravel patch out front.

He stormed back into the kitchen with renewed fervour, foraging the walls for a previously undetected inlet. The cupboards were all wrong, with some budged off center and others disassembled and grouped to the sides.

Leo crisscrossed their web and came to face a modest, draped passageway carved roughly into the stonework. Lighting a fresh candlestick fetched from one of the cupboards, he descended below ground, partial to the earthiness of raw cellars and unbothered by their stale, wet air, which he soaked up with unprecedented glee. The tight space proved to hold bountiful provisions, and Leo shuffled the sacks of grain to reveal a dusty trapdoor underneath. Inside was a chest, unlocked and full of spoils.

It dawned on him that this was much too easy. He could reconcile the improbability of the unmanned grounds, for in this restricted, holy place, the nuns themselves were likely ignorant

148

to any of the ruse; he was even willing to buy the farcical grapevine through which this location was magically disclosed. It was the timing and eagerness with which his dear partners dispatched him here that stunk of an epic setup. He blasted himself for his mind-numbing nonchalance, for being so wrapped up in the arrogance of his own mental adroitness that he did not casually stumble into this trap, oh no, he gaily waltzed into it.

Somebody upstairs wanted him to hang, all right, and why? What real threat did he pose to anyone in the business aside from his incessant thirst to get out?

He was a sitting duck and, upon walking out with the loot, a marked man. In that respect, it hardly mattered if he took the bait; he was marked regardless. Leo snuck a handful of banknotes and let out an unceremonious snort. In their slapdash plan of ultimate sabotage, the dullards overlooked his strongest forte of dealing in counterfeit. While fond of hocking the real riches, he was more than proficient in dealing the fakes, and this lousy paper was better suited for monopoly money. He giggled uncontrollably, supposing the lightweight bullion were no more than convincingly wrapped bars of Swiss chocolate.

Unclear on his next course of action, Leo withdrew from the inn empty-handed, planning to lay low until he could sort out a strategy to disappear or, if he felt up to it, plot revenge.

Treading softly along the stone fence adjacent to his courtyard, he sensed activity on the other side. Were they waiting for him this whole time? Could it be his end? He paused and listened as twigs rustled under his feet, making the stranger, or strangers, aware of his presence.

There was an alternative gate in that wall, and Leo considered using it for a last minute ambush. If he were to go out, he wanted to make the identities of his assailants known. And yet, a subdued intuitiveness told him that his supposed adversaries were more unsettled by him than he was by them. Shrouded in dead silence, he edged forth timidly, eventually slipping out onto Ril'sky Lane and resolving to circle the estate in order to enter his courtyard from the far end.

The roundabout walk took nearly fifteen minutes, convincing Leo the parties across the wall had to have scurried off by then. As a precaution, he coasted in the shadows of the courtyard, converging on the maintenance sheds where someone stood not long ago. The probability of their persisting presence was slim, but he kept his guard, espying a sequestered corner under the weeping willows. He sloped against the crisp bark, closed his eyes, and tuned into the quiet. Although there was nothing alien within it, he did not feel sufficiently alone.

Another fifteen minutes elapsed, and he started to doze before being alerted to a scuttle in his proximity. He propped himself up, zeroing in on the visible stretch of dirt between the sheds. He saw a person of small stature, an adolescent girl, fussing in the shrub and, to his astonishment, dragging out a human figure, motionless and remarkably dead. There was something familiar in her body language; he swore he had seen her before, watching as she struggled with the dead weight, lugging it back toward their complex. She was going for the basement, and he crawled ahead wary of making a sound, for if she was spooked, the thrilling show could be compromised.

In an instance, a ray of light from the cathedral's bell tower exposed her features, and Leo choked back an exclamation at the startling reveal of her identity; it was none other than his young niece. His gut urged him to embrace her, shield her, and aid her, yet there was no context to the actions he witnessed. Who was the deceased? Did she have a hand in his death, or was it a cover-up for somebody else, and if so, what monster pressured his darling girl into something this wretched?

Leo waited patiently as she vanished in the basement and emerged shortly without the body. He watched her sort out the tools by the sheds and sweep up, no doubt impairing any excess evidence.

Given the impression she had left for good, he entered the basement's narrow, foul-smelling corridor. With only his lighter as guidance, he bumped around, coming to distinguish a body laid out on the floor of the chute room. He crouched beside it and lowered his lighter.

"Well, how about that, old lad?" he sneered aloud.

Sasha Bandura was a blacklisted, filthy twerp who thought too highly of himself and had no place in the business. His penchant for young things was common knowledge, and it was not until he dared solicit children from wealthier neighbourhoods such as this one that a vote was taken to phase out his involvement. Sensing inevitable exposure and exile, the creep ensured himself by weaving numerous, and many a time, unsuspecting parties into his web of deceit. In the event of an execution, he devised to leave behind a plethora of loose ends, people whose sheer existence would be cause for concern irrelevant of what they actually knew, and not even the most hardened of bosses wanted to start down that path, for it was unclear just how steep the body count could get.

This insipid weasel had managed to get the heavyweights by the balls, manipulating his way to immunity, a point that angered Leo in his own ostensibly futile quest to dodge the crosshairs. He leaned in, relishing the maimed facial features, the savagery of the slashed throat, the rigour of the kill, and the degrading stark nakedness of the body, serving as a grim reminder of perseverance in the oft-precarious game of survival. On this ill-boding night, Leo took considerable comfort in the solid infallibility that the body displayed in front of him was not his own.

Chapter 18

Chuchin and Komarovsky were scrambling to make sense of a fresh case handed to them on short notice by the captain who, as rumour had it, owed a favour to the father of the family involved.

The precinct was expected to put on a great show of competency and swiftness in order to oblige its new, high-rolling customer. This was the modern climate they lived in, where men with a bit of spare cash could call upon officers of the law in much the same fashion they would a mechanic or a plumber, anticipating first-rate service with guaranteed satisfaction.

Aiding crooks on demand was becoming a bankable business with no shortage of money to be made. Real crimes had taken a back seat; there was no room for everyday folk, for honesty, for efficient police work, or anything that even hinted at the truth. Bribes and special favours were prevalent since days of yore, but it was the unapologetic boldness with which the affairs were presently conducted that set them apart from anything previously seen.

The toxicity of this dizzying mayhem had thrown Chuchin into a tizzy. Fed up and keen on quitting the dog and pony show, he was building up the nerve to tell Komarovsky, who had not fared much better, though still strove to hold down the fort.

Their new case made for initial confusion as the detectives were contacted about an Inna Dvorkina, whose abduction took place in the farthest corner of the Left Bank and way out of their jurisdiction. Their attention was called to the girl's extracurricular activities, specifically, her enrolment at the Opera's dance academy where she attended rehearsals with Sasha Bandura and a string of youngsters, who were later found to have been molested by him.

Granted, she did not appear to be among the abused; they supposed it an intriguing coincidence. Ordinarily, coincidences made for weak links, but this was Dvorkin's show now, and the captain was positive these chance parallels would reignite Komarovsky's interest.

Chuchin indeed saw a revived enthusiasm in his partner, who rationalized Inna to have dodged Bandura's advances because of her age, in that by the time he settled within the academy's walls, she had outgrown his desires, becoming too physically mature for his liking.

On the other hand, her father was waist deep in money laundering, both then and now, making a ploy of vindictive extortion all the more conceivable, aside from the glaring omission of a ransom six days into the kidnapping. With no concrete leads, and hours passed rapidly into days, the family and the precinct were at a loss for an explanation.

Komarovsky thought Dvorkin to be quite a character, one who arranged a cushy emigration to Hungary as early as December, were the paperwork to clear in time. He was a shining example of the kind of excess money could buy and how effortlessly it was rendered useless. Here he was, caught unawares, clueless as to who took his daughter and why. His connections were skin deep and came up short, suggesting this was the work of real die-hards, the criminal elite, who had no need for his money or anything else he was willing to pledge.

Having drained his private channels, he now rallied on official ones, looking to Chuchin and Komarovsky to bleed their moles dry. According to Dvorkin, all bottom feeders could be bought for the right price, and he was ready to pay by the word, concurrently offering the detectives the biggest payout of their careers, were they to succeed in this endeavour.

All they needed was a tipoff, and it came in the form of Klara Feldblum. Dvorkin's sources claimed she was with Inna during the abduction and happened to get away, giving no reason as to why they were there in the first place. The girls made for a strange pair; they were not friends, nor were their families particularly cozy, yet they were close enough to venture far from home, in secrecy, and without rational motive. Moreover, Klara was one of the abused, and her brother Yakov had long been a suspect in Bandura's disappearance, albeit no credible evidence was ever gathered to prove it.

The more coincidences they aimed to establish, the less sense any of it made. How could Dvorkin's sources know where and by what means Inna was taken, while staying oblivious to the identity of her aggressors? How could they know about Klara's presence, had they not been there themselves; or if they genuinely did shake the stoolies, why alert them to this seemingly ineffectual detail?

"Because it's not ineffectual," Komarovsky uttered at last.

"I've just about had it," said Chuchin. "This is turning into a déjà vu, into that same web of shit where they cover each other's arses, and we've not the slightest clue which rogues are spinning it."

"The payout looks good, doesn't it?"

"It would look better if we had a real chance at nabbing it."

"You think he won't pay?"

"Oh, he'll pay. It's just that we can't deliver."

"We just might, Chuch. I've got a feeling about this one."

"You had a feeling about the last one, too, a trifling missing persons we couldn't crack."

"No, not trifling. They are connected, you'll see, maybe not in the way we think or we'd like, but they are. If we solve this one, the other will solve itself. I'm sure of it."

"Great. So what now, dear Zheglov?"

"We visit the Feldblums. That girl holds the key," replied Komarovsky, convincing Chuchin that his partner was better at playing detective than being one. Their exchanges read like reruns of police procedurals, complete with obligatory red herrings, false suspects, locked-room mysteries, and imminent twists. They dressed the part, drove the car, smoked the Marlboros, and roughed up a hooligan or two on occasion to sustain credibility. What a farce it was, but all in good fun.

The detectives' sojourn with Yakov and Klara Feldblum proved most illuminating, as it introduced a new player into their ever-changing calamity of a case. Dessa Faustova was said to also be present during Inna's abduction, her involvement expertly omitted by Dvorkin's informers. Klara would have omitted it, too, had Yakov not blurted out a damning phrase of "the trio," setting in motion a series of inquiries neither Feldblum could ignore.

Chuchin and Komarovsky were then reminded of May's Opera House recital in which the girls performed together as soloists. Klara and Inna's lack of friendship notwithstanding, it was Dessa who nurtured an amicable companionship with both and was the glue holding their circle together. Klara surmised it was childish curiosity that incited the girls to venture out on the Left Bank and meander parts of the city their parents so ardently forbade them to visit. There was nothing else to it, she claimed, no secrets, no conspiracy, none that they were aware of, at least.

When asked why she and Dessa were spared, Klara proposed that Inna was made vulnerable, having strayed from the pack as they gained ground, a fatal misjudgement that distanced them from her attack and obscured the enemy.

At last, the facts were shaping into something tangible, or maybe it was yet another smokescreen. In this puzzle, facts and their tangibility were relative, noncommittal entities, and Komarovsky did not rule out the dire possibility that they were, in effect, being skilfully guided farther away from the truth. The Faustov household would be their next stop, and the detectives chose to pursue it at once so as not to give Klara a chance to warn her friend of their impending drop in.

Scaling several flights of stairs, they were greeted by the lady of the house. She had little to add in her understanding of what transpired, aside from grumbling about the "savages" who injured her daughter, a second detail that comfortably slipped Dvorkin's pigeons, and the duo asked themselves how many more of these unaccounted-for details there were.

Mother led them to Dessa's room, thinking the brat would be forced to break her silence when faced with the threat of real authority.

Napping at her secretary, Dessa gained consciousness at the sound of alien footsteps nearing her room. There were three sets, the routine childish stomp of Mother and those of two clumsy baboons, who must have rarely bothered to pick up their feet and straighten their postures, schlepping their soiled, heavy stumps on the newly polished parquet. The door jerked without a knock, and Mother introduced the unwelcome guests, disclosing Dessa's current condition as one of shock and considerable stress.

"We decided to let her continue studies from home, until she's well enough to rejoin her classmates."

"You and your husband?"

"No, my father and I."

Komarovsky nodded with sympathy and pulled up a stool.

"The front legs wobble," said Dessa. "I'd be careful."

"Duly noted. I've got some questions for you, dear. You can call me Komar, and back there is my partner, Chuchin."

"Won't you offer them tea, Mother?" she replied, uninterested in their introductions. She knew who they were. What she could not stand, however, was another minute of Mother's smugness. The witch must have readied for a juicy reveal, expecting her to fold like a cheap suit in the company of intimidating flatfoots.

"No such luck," the girl mumbled.

"Pardon?"

"What is it you want to ask? I've much homework to do."

"We'd like to know your side of the story."

"My side?"

"Regarding Inna Dvorkina's kidnapping, that is."

"Yes, of course. What other side is there?"

"We've come from the Feldblums'. Your friend Klara told us all there was."

Finding their amateur tactics nothing short of astonishing, Dessa confirmed the blubbering louses to have no grasp on elite psychological trickery reminiscent of Porfiry Petrovich.

"You don't say, then why are you questioning me?"

Chuchin and Komarovsky were visibly dumbfounded.

"You said Klara told you everything, so why does my 'side' of it matter?"

Mother returned with a silver tray of freshly brewed drinks and biscotti.

"We need to corroborate your stories," grunted Chuchin as he was handed a delicate teacup and saucer.

"I'm afraid I can't tell you any more than you already know. I was dealt a hard blow to the mouth and head, you see. I can't recall much of anything since then."

"What about before then? Do you remember the attack?"

"Mine or Inna's?"

"Either."

"She fell behind as we walked the deserted street. A car must have waited nearby, because as soon as we were separated, she was ambushed."

"And then they chased after you?"

"No, I chased after them."

"How many were there?"

"Two, and at least one in the car."

"What kind of car was it?"

"A black Volga."

"Did you struggle with them?"

"No, I was hit beforehand."

"And they just left you?"

"It would seem so."

"Where was Klara?"

"Up ahead, I guess."

"She chose not to intervene?"

"I'm not sure it was a question of choice."

"How so?"

"The paralysis of fear. Couldn't budge if she wanted to."

"So that makes you the brave one."

"Or the stupid one, depending on where you're standing."

"Were you taken to a hospital?"

"No, so I was told."

"Then you were taken straight home?"

"Apparently."

"By whom?"

"Couldn't tell you."

"That's interesting. Klara couldn't tell us, either."

They turned to Mother. "What about you, Lady Faustova? Can you tell us how your daughter made it home?"

"They rang the doorbell and left her."

"They?"

"Those who brought her up. Don't ask any more, as I don't know. That's your job, detectives."

Komarovsky fidgeted on the stool, sipping his tea. "Yes, hmm. One last question. Why were you girls there in the first place?"

"That's what I've been trying to get out of her for a week," chimed in Mother.

"We like to take trips sometimes."

"Trips?"

"On the metro. We'd go to the farthest stops of the lines and wander about."

"You can bet that's not going to happen again," Mother said, theatrically wagging her finger.

"Klara was adamant this was your only time."

"I would be, too, had Yakov stood over me."

"We didn't say he was there," pointed out Chuchin.

"Oh, but he was, and she was trying to save face."

"How many such trips did you take?"

"A handful."

"And you never had a specific destination in mind?"

"No, as long as we didn't stray too far from the station."

"Alright," exhaled Komarovsky, closing his notepad and securing it in the pocket of his worn leather bomber. "That'll be all for now. We do reserve the right to come back, if required."

"As you please."

"I'll see you men out," said Mother, motioning them into the corridor. "And you, cheeky runt," she turned to Dessa, "you and I aren't finished."

Komarovsky crunched on a mouthful of biscotti, stuffing his giant palms with whatever he could fit.

"That's just it," he said suddenly, washing down his makeshift meal with the last of the tea.

159

Dessa looked up from her papers.

"Inna was kidnapped around Tumanovskaya Lane, and that is extremely far from any station, metro or otherwise, at least a half hour's walk."

He shrugged, making a show of how cursory the idea was. Wiping crumbs entrenched in the corners of his mouth and smearing his hands on his trousers, he dawdled out of the room.

Dessa was elated; her eyes twinkled. Not bad, she thought. This one had potential; but with only brief glimpses of mental agility, neither he nor his partner was going to solve her, much less get close to Uncle Leo, who was a bona fide virtuoso of stealth, unyielding, and phantasmal.

ಠ

Mother plodded around the foyer, rubbing her palms together as if to summon the aid of an ulterior force. Having learned a bare fraction of what she suspected to be the real truth, she cursed the cantankerous child for driving her to the brink of madness. In a short instant, she cared not about acquiring answers, with her intense hunger to know warping into a burning sensation of malevolence. That behaviour, the audacity to question authority and demean the rules of the household, was unacceptable, and Mother was bent on stripping Dessa of her precious liberties in order to teach her a valuable lesson in obedience and humility.

In the kitchen, Dessa scoured the refrigerator for hearty afternoon refreshments, having exhausted her energy on the cat and mouse game she so enjoyed. A slapping with a verbal tirade was imminent, and trying to hold off on it would prolong the perverse pleasure Mother took in the wait of eventually dishing it out, a pleasure Dessa was not about to grant.

"Ungrateful girl, what makes you think you can embarrass me this way?" shouted Mother, approaching from the foyer and furious, as expected.

"I've done nothing wrong, and they haven't got a clue."

"These little strolls of yours, they are no more."

"That's fine; I've lost interest in them, anyhow."

"Have you lost interest in the Jewess as well? Because I won't let you see her again."

"We go to the same academy, Mother, it's unavoidable."

"In that case, one of you is going to transfer."

"I'm too promising to dance anywhere else, not to mention the stain such a gesture would leave on the family name."

"I wasn't talking about you."

"Arrange what you like."

"What am I to tell everyone, Dessa?"

"About what?"

"People have been talking."

"What people, Mother?"

"I want to know what you told Leo."

"The same thing I told the detectives."

"Liar! Those were just stories."

"No, Mother. Those stories happen to be the truth."

"If you defy me again, I won't spare you."

Dessa lowered her head and relaxed her body, as tensing up would only hurt more. She visualized the impact of Mother's forearm on her temple, her jaw, or maybe her shoulder. Every instance, and there were many, carried on as an out-of-body experience. She watched herself being thrown around, dragged about corridors, locked in closets, sometimes made to eat her meals in the stairwell, had she been lucky to get any at all. Threats and physical punishment had no effect whatsoever, and Mother had started using food as the ultimate tool of power. The hit never came, and when Dessa opened her eyes, Mother was setting out plates at the kitchen table.

"Let's forget about it," she said, her tone suddenly obliging and softened. "You look hungry."

Nodding in agreement, Dessa pulled up a chair. "What will you make?"

"How about some porridge?"

"I suppose that'll do."

"Good."

The change was no doubt suspicious, but Dessa's stomach could take no more as she spied Mother comb the cabinets for the last of the farina, switch on the gas, and put on a small pot of milk. Scrutinizing her empty plate, she fantasized about Shurik's luncheons and dinner parties with tables on the verge of collapse from the weight of savoury cheeses, lush platters of ripe Azerbaijani pomegranates, and pitchers of full-bodied Georgian wines. It was a glorious image not unlike her favourite paintings of Roman banquets and religious feasts, albeit meals with Mother were more suggestive of The Feast of Herod than anything else.

The pot came to a boil. Without setting it aside to cool even a moment, Mother diligently filled their plates with steaming slop.

Handed her share, Dessa sloshed it around with a spoon, hoping the mass would stay down once consumed. Before she could give it a taste, Mother swatted the spoon out of her hand, plucked her by the hair, and thrust her head into the hot porridge.

Dessa howled in pain, her face scalded and sore. The woman held still, pushing her farther. Arduously, she wormed her way out of Mother's grip and slid to the floor, gasping for air. Mother coldly looked on.

"Clean yourself up," she said. "I don't allow swine at my table."

Dessa rose slowly and silently, ready for a second fit of temper. None came. Limping out of the kitchen and into the bathroom, she took special care to wipe away the thick coating

162

of grout that had dripped down her neck and soiled her clothes. The shrill of the running tap mellowed her sobs. It was all so cruel, even for Mother. Dessa reckoned there was some justice in it, as she deliberately egged the witch on day in and day out, challenging her own breaking point, curious as to which of Mother's countless outbursts would trigger her mania. The rage had taken hold of her once, and she knew it would, without fail, manifest again, given the proper circumstances.

Chapter 19

Mother was determined to end the year on a high note and nothing, especially not this unforeseen nuisance with Dessa, was going to deter her from realizing her first physical encounter with Chuck Bedford, who was scheduled for a month-long stay in December. The girl was home-schooled for most of November, but Mother had yet to tell her of Chuck's forthcoming arrival. First impressions were of utmost importance, and it was crucial to get her daughter under control.

Chuck's meet-and-greet was a one-time deal and a deciding factor of their future together. Those from the marriage agency who had already reeled in their American princes were emphatic that, were a man passionate about his stay, a proposal would surely follow before his departure. Had there been no proposal by that deadline, the partnership was a lost cause, and the planning of such visits would have to start afresh with a different fellow. A daunting assignment, considering Mother had stacked all of her chips in Chuck's favour and possessed not the slightest emotional will to start the search over.

She was weary of generic letters and uncouth telephone chatter, of playing into the fantasy of an obedient Slavic maiden, whose chief hope was to turn submissive for an overtly egotistic, iron-handed Yank. Mother distained these "princes," for they were anything but; yet younger women flocked to them as if they were saviours of the weaker sex. She was relieved to see Chuck as a different breed of man. He, unlike the domineering bulk, was true freedom in disguise.

Preparations included consulting an itinerary of tourist attractions, as Mother believed falling in love with the city was key in igniting amorous feelings toward her. Some women proposed the opposite to be true, resolving to boost the drabness of their dwellings and committing to advertise little more than stereotypes of post-Soviet disintegration pockmarking the city's bereft landscapes. The more substandard their quality of life appeared in comparison, the quicker their cavaliers would act in plucking them out of their misery.

Mother's name afforded her a rare fortuity to strive a tad higher, having no use for tricks or distortions, for they were not her truth, and there was no reason to pass them off as such. She was more than willing to showcase her riches, respectability, and social status in return for a chance to actively participate in the Western tradition, one that had no semblance to the Soviet mentality of strife and eternal suffering. If she were his East, then Chuck was her West, and Mother was compelled for the twain to form a lifelong, lasting bond.

ಸಃ

10 December 1992 marked Chuck's anticipated arrival in Kiev. Mother and Shurik rode to Borispol airport to pick him up while Dessa eagerly kept watch at home. She was informed of his visit not a week prior, ecstatic with the promise of a brand-new face joining their household. Most of all, she looked forward to a period of tranquillity, because Mother would not dare brandish her temper in front of a suitor. Upon receiving a call notifying her of Chuck's safe landing, she had upward of an hour to set a

welcome table and brew a pot of coffee for their guest. Thinking he would be fatigued and grungy from his laborious journey, she laid out a fresh set of towels, fluffing the mattress and pillows in the spare room where he was to sleep.

The call came. Chuck was well, and the group was heading home. Dessa set out their finest porcelain, arranged the food platters in record time, and made comfortable on a shoe bench in the foyer, her eyes fixed on the main door. She kept that way for a quarter of an hour and began to doze, floating through a pitch-dark hallway before finding herself back in the kitchen.

The table was cleared, with just a kettle whistling on the stove. In spite of being right there in front of her, it whistled somewhere in great distance, and Dessa had to administer the whole of her physical strength to switch off the burner. The flat stood undisturbed, with Mother lurking about, ripe to materialize in a flash, were she summoned by Dessa's subconscious. The girl was meticulously setting an afternoon silver tea service for one, arranging the tray, placing three sugar cubes to the left of the saucer as Mother fancied sucking on them whilst sipping her tea. From under the sink, she recovered a packet of rat poison, dividing its contents evenly between the teapot and the creamer. Using sugar tongs to give them a good whirl, she called on Mother without as much as a word escaping her lips.

Impassive to the spectacle about to initiate, Dessa walked out of their apartment and rode the elevator to the basement. Mindful it was not the same elevator or even the same basement, she traversed the unfamiliar maze to discover herself amidst ruins of a sidelined construction project. Scanning the site for signs of life, she was assured of its ghostly vacancy. Rows of cement bags mounted before her, enticing the girl to enter their proximity. A lone tug revealed them to be totally weightless, illogically so, and Dessa stacked them like books, willing several batches worth back to the flat.

166

In the kitchen, Mother's body was sprawled out on a rug beneath the table with arms and legs twisted abnormally as if frozen in the midst of a severe convulsion. Foaming at the mouth with eyes slightly open, her expression insinuated a state of unconsciousness instead of irreversible death. Unaffected by the ghoulish sight, Dessa moved into her bedroom and hauled out a medium-sized clothing trunk, a keepsake handed down by Shurik that he professed her prematurely deceased grandmother was determined to pass on. And so it was passed on, though she found little use for it until now. Consistently locked, the trunk stood open, appearing bottomless and inviting.

Dessa retreated to the kitchen and took hold of Mother's right leg, towing her smoothly into the bedroom. The woman was under paralysis; while her mind functioned sufficiently enough to understand the inevitable, she was physically unable to intervene. Unceremoniously disposed of in the trunk, she waited for the small space to go dark. Instead, Dessa reached for a large pitcher, liberally pouring its contents into the crate. A cold, oozing substance coated Mother's incapacitated body as stacks of cement bags morphed into rows of pitchers, which she emptied leisurely, one by one.

A voice was calling out, not Mother's, a strong, safe, masculine voice Dessa never had the pleasure of hearing before. She squirmed, tossing awake from her delusion. Mother would live another day, saved by Chuck's good graces.

"Afternoon, dear. I'm delighted to finally meet you," he said, extending his weathered hands.

She clung to his strapping arms, allowing him to sweep her up into a tender embrace. His shirt collar carried faint aromas of tobacco and crisp, woody cologne, a scent Dessa quickly patented as that of a cowboy. Mother hovered over them, placing one hand on the girl's temple and the other on Chuck's shoulder, giving both a soft rub. With each passing moment that his affection grew in its authenticity, hers was exposed as all the more fake.

"What an absolute doll!" he cheered. "I've got a gift hidden somewhere in here for you."

The foyer was crowded with suitcases and tote bags. Shurik handed out house slippers while Mother busied herself in the kitchen, knowing full well there was not a thing left to do, for the welcome table was flawless, and yet she fussed, jumbling drawers and clanking silverware.

"Don't bother with that now, the gifts can wait," she said with a startling, heavy accent, but Chuck continued his search.

A hard leather portmanteau disclosed a decoratively wrapped box and was promptly handed to Dessa. She dove in and removed a pair of snow-white roller skates with ruby pink wheels. Every bit of them was wondrous and spellbinding.

"You like?"

"Why yes! They are delightful! How can I thank you?"

"Enjoy them."

"I certainly will!"

He pulled her in and gave her head a kiss.

"Your English seems much better than hers," he giggled.

Dessa beamed. The two of them were getting on swimmingly.

A full hour of food, drink, and broken gabble rounded off with Shurik excusing himself back to his flat, a tour of which was available as early as the following afternoon, had their guest expressed interest. Chuck would spend the rest of the evening settling into his quarters as Mother sorted his luggage. Dessa scrutinized each dress shirt Mother laid on the sofa.

He brought five in total, all long sleeved, three made of denim and two of tartan. The white one, with red piping, lavish embroidery and an intricate yoke, was, presumably, his Sunday's best. There were hats, a fringed jacket, two pairs of boots, one cowhide, one alligator, blue jeans, bolo ties, and belt buckles, the biggest of which was said to have been won in a rodeo; all in all, an assortment of garb that worked like a Western costume outlet, rather than everyday wear.

Chuck's chronicles of ranching, horse riding, and rodeos captivated Dessa. She envisaged the fairs, the petting zoos, the infinite tents of lemonade, sweets, and fried oddities that sounded nothing short of divine, a world entirely contrary to her own and all the more bewitching.

Mother was keen on him. Dessa was absolutely smitten. She wanted him to stay forever, and if that was not possible, for him to take her away. Would he fall for Mother in the end, really fall for her, the way men fell for women on the telly, professing their love in monologues to soaring violins under soft lighting? She found it hard to believe any man could foster that kind of warmth and passion for a woman who lacked either, her disposition primarily rigid and manipulative. By no means did the few friends Mother managed to acquire stick around for years out of sheer pleasure for her company; some were loyal, others were smart, hoping to ride her coattails had she ever struck big in business or love. It was success by association, and Chuck was, first and foremost, a business settlement.

&.

The last week of December was spent at the Faustov dacha in Boyarka, where the family geared up to ring in the New Year. Their cottage underwent cosmetic renovations several weeks prior to Chuck's arrival, with Mother sprucing up the attic and updating amenities to impress her admirer. The dacha and its land were not only demonstrative of the family's affluence, but also of a culture suitably in sync with Chuck's way of being. He saw them as city dwellers perfectly alert to the pitfalls of metropolitan life and, for this reason, consciously choosing to set aside a time and place to participate in a kind of togetherness with nature. He identified it most acutely in the young girl, who was euphoric to leave the city behind, not in a straightforward, childlike sense, but in a precisely adult manner of dodging a demon, a darkness that had taken over all there was, and the only means of escape was by retreating back into something natural, pure, and untarnished. The two played together daily, skating on the frozen pond in the mornings and riding toboggans in the afternoons. In the evenings, they lounged before a blazing fireplace in total silence as she rested her head on his rhythmically swelling chest. Chuck made time for Mother and Shurik, for he grew to cherish the family as a whole; yet she, this precious, vulnerable girl and the bond they developed from the onset, was what he treasured most.

Likewise, this grouping was Dessa's perception of an ideal, if not entirely orthodox, family unit, and Chuck's steadfast presence was the guaranteed end to her longstanding, intimate nightmare that was life with Mother. Shurik tended to tread those grounds carefully. Concerned for Dessa, he also believed in minding his own affairs and rarely interfered beyond occasionally voicing his displeasure at Mother's gratuitous harshness. Leo was the true champion of standing up to her, but he was not around in the required capacity to make the potency of his masculinity known and properly feared. Had he seen what Mother was really up to, he would have crippled her without so much as a wink, and knowing that, she made sure to engage in her vilest abuse on the days he was out of everyone's reach.

Dessa missed Uncle Leo, and she mused that he and Chuck would make friends just as comfortably. On the off chance they did not, Leo would find their guest a great laugh, a caricature of the Wild West he could flaunt in his circles, passing on the torch of being the family's professional fool.

In the meantime, he was back in the city ironing out the kinks of Inna's homecoming after a month of negotiations turned sour. For Dessa, Inna's return had become a dubious concept. Uncle

Leo professed she was quite alive and unharmed, providing no answer as to what was being done to her or where. She had to bathe, eat, drink and clothe, and the mob was not running a bed and breakfast, so it struck Dessa as far-fetched that gritty, legitimate gangsters would busy themselves with such trivial, time-consuming responsibilities. A more credible projection would have Inna locked up in an isolated warehouse, starving, and unkempt at best.

The girl believed wholeheartedly in Leo's claims of Inna's aliveness. It was the rest that did not make sense. He refused to disclose the men's motivation for taking her and turned mighty irritable whenever she brought it up. He became jittery at the mention of detectives making their rounds and was overly concerned about police involvement in general, oblivious to the fact that no one had attempted to make contact or seemed remotely interested in his whereabouts. The detectives were onto something, yes, but their theories, no matter how valid and proximate to scratching the surface of truth, had no chance of being substantiated. Other cases would come, supplemented by bodies, rapes, thefts, and missing persons with more enigmatic suspects, incomprehensible circumstances, and disturbing motives, making this one just another unsolved mystery qualified to gather dust on a decrepit shelf in the precinct's leak-prone basement archives. The system, ceasing to function justly in the ongoing environment of roaming excess and limitless opportunity, was on the brink of full-scale implosion; it would be a miracle to locate the file at all a year from now, much less recall its contents or harp on its pending status.

A fleeting suspicion hit Dessa one morning about the true nature of Inna's kidnapping. She was never their intended prey. The mysterious girl with no name, whom Dessa found uncanny in resemblance to Inna, was likely the target. If it were true that this criminal network always kept watch, someone could have

171

easily sighted their brief exchange and snitched up the ladder. An order was given to make her vanish. By the time the cavalry arrived, she was long gone and in the safety of her mother's flat. In the blinding darkness, the goons mistook Inna for the tattletale. An honest blunder, but had it been the case, which sounded more probable than anything Uncle Leo was willing to divulge, their mistake would be realized in a jiffy, meriting an expeditious return of the wrong merchandise to its rightful owner. In spite of the misunderstanding, Dvorkin would still cough up a ransom, a winning scenario the criminals had no desire to milk, thereby retaining Inna and disregarding her father's sizeable assets. The situation was deadlocked, its agenda obscured from the start. Somebody in the chain of command was lying, and it was only a matter of time before the lie and its liar were unearthed.

Chapter 20

The year was 1993. The first days of this enchanting period were strongest in their emotional astuteness. They were promising of permanent change in the unfaltering quest of self-improvement, encouraging in the way of goals and resolutions. Dessa was swept by a wave of contagious optimism. Everyone was.

The family was heading back to the city, bringing to a close Chuck's last week of stay. They would celebrate Orthodox Christmas together, and soon afterwards, he would be gone. The atmosphere was not like that of the May Day holidays where people deserted the city in hopes of breaking from restraints of civilization. Quite the opposite, strangers longed for the warmth of each other's company. Their bodies huddled downtown, walked the streets, and circled the imperial Nordmann fir erected annually in the Independence Square.

They were to stop at Shurik's for afternoon tea before returning to Mother's apartment. As their chauffeur pulled to the building, Dessa was overtaken by frantic discomfort.

The area was too quiet, the air too crisp, the trottoir too sanded, the entrances too groomed, the Finnish guards too stylized; it was all too something, and yet nothing in particular.

This visibly unnoticeable change had taken place in their absence and was akin to a bad gut feeling people customarily observed in dangerous, uncharted territory. The building's aura was skewed beyond the original crime Dessa had committed; a different moral breach had taken place and with drastically graver consequences. It felt recent, enormous, and shocking.

Set to reunite in fifteen minutes, Shurik and Dessa took the stairs while Chuck and Mother rode the elevator to her flat for a baggage drop-off and a sprightly wash-up. Shurik led, closing in on the front door, when Dessa saw it was not sealed shut, suggesting someone had fled in a hurry. She watched her grandfather cautiously push it open. Her discomfort intensified.

"Hold on, darling," he said, creeping forward.

She heard his soft steps fade, and with each pressing minute of silence, willed herself to proceed.

The drawn curtains allowed for minimal illumination, and Shurik had yet to turn on a single light fixture. He was down the corridor in the dining room. Already, Dessa felt a striking spatial void. Things were missing. The foyer's walls that, mere weeks ago, held copious Venetian mirrors, were now bare. The hallway was rid of its exclusive paintings, and she glided her fingertips over the hooks on which they used to hang.

Shurik's dining room had him cowering on the parquet, for there were no chairs, no tables, and no rugs. Dessa reached for the light switch but, glancing up, saw no chandelier. She drew open the curtains to face the lone piece of furniture, a sprawling china cabinet too cumbersome for a hasty carry-out. With interiors identically hollow, its shelves were stripped clean of antique porcelain, fine crystal, and royal silverware.

Dessa bolted to the library and, switching on a torchiere, was met with cleared bookshelves. The club chair and nine-foot Blüthner were sole survivors, with the former unworthy of a steep payout and the latter too complicated to dismantle.

She headed to Uncle Leo's room to check on the baby grand Ibach. It was removed, along with a chiffonier and a piano bench. His sculpting station was wiped clean, leaving no signs of the White Guard.

Panicked and whimpering, she went back to the dining room.

"Everything is gone, Grandpapa."

His head hung low. He did not answer.

There were footsteps in the main hallway. Mother and Chuck were on their way. They entered the apartment, and Dessa heard them fuss about, undoubtedly taken by surprise. After a brief pause, their footsteps rushed through the corridor, and all were united.

"There is nothing left, Mama. Not here, not anywhere."

Mother heaved a shallow sigh, grasping at the wall behind her. She scanned the barren room and fell to her knees in disbelief. Chuck tended to her as best he could, but she was inconsolable, finally acknowledging Shurik across the room and mustering what strength she had to crawl over.

"Father!" she screamed, rattling his shoulders. "My God, Father, talk to me!"

She lifted his head. He was unresponsive and pale. His eyes had turned to stone with arms and legs twisting into one another like vines.

"Call the police, Dessa!" she yelled, and the girl hustled to where the telephone used to be. It was not there. Mother was raving.

"Try the kitchen one!"

Dessa obliged. Met with the same thin outline on a dusty stand, she returned empty-handed.

"It's vanished like the rest."

"Run upstairs, use ours! And take him with you," Mother said, pointing at Chuck.

Consenting to her orders, they abandoned the flat.

175

"Please, Father," she begged. "Say something, anything! Oh, my dear Papa. Who could have done this?"

"Leo," he muttered at last. "It was Leo."

Chapter 21

The dicey abduction of Inna Dvorkina added to Leo's headache of dealings within his crime branch. On and off since May, he concocted a scheme to avenge himself and defraud his treacherous partners, whose demise at his hands would grant him partial access to the head honchos. He assessed it feasible to take down a pair at best, for they would be replaced tout de suite and with a heavy dose of rancour. By that time, however, he would be little more than an afterthought. He established himself early on as someone who could not be swayed by familial ties, and smoking him out by taking loved ones hostage would prove fruitless. It was a well-crafted facade, of course, but Leo was so sure to have convinced the branch of his ruthlessness that he was riding on the pure chance no one would dare try.

As it happened, just when he dug to the bottom of things regarding his own predicament, going so far as to finalize a conceivable plan of action, his niece called upon him with a plea of her own. It was an incredible coincidence that she and her friends were to find the address book he so imprudently lost sight of one morning on his way to a meeting. Whatever Dessa thought she uncovered, his importance in the matter was grossly overestimated, for he, quite literally and plainly, was the book's keeper and not a smidgen more. Leo never participated in the kidnapping of women or their subsequent trade into the industry. His single requirement was providing addresses for partners who were later made to keep tabs on families left behind, paying sporadic visits to the rowdier kin as a reminder they were still on notice.

The inconvenient loss of his records was in no terms an irreparable cataclysm, in that the scribbles would be rendered a meaningless summary of locations to anyone who came in contact with them. Leo never let on of his mishap, and it was not until last winter that a cohort from a budding offshoot recorded a pattern of familiar faces frequenting his stakeouts.

In this case, life was exercising a sense of humour, having led a lost item into the hands of his inordinately inquisitive niece, who took it upon herself to play city detective with a couple of girlfriends.

When a day of elementary surveillance traced the identities of the young culprits, Leo was informed of Dessa's prying eyes. He was unwavering in assuring the cohort it was child's play and posed no risk to anyone's operations, a stray exposure of personal interest he worried would not go unrecognized. Luckily, their visits became sparse and, for a spell, ceased altogether, or so he had hoped. The girls resurfaced after months of inaction, making the mistake of verbally engaging a family, whose members fatally reciprocated the trio's interest. So went the official story, at least, and it was this cohort who chose to bypass Dessa on the night of Dvorkina's kidnapping, tipping off his network of backups to pick her up and deliver her home. The man knew his merciful act would reach Leo, and when it did, they would enter into an unspoken, binding contract of give-and-take.

He cursed the untimely business with Inna for making him deviate from his plans. Except, as he burrowed deeper into the wicked labyrinth of Kiev's expanding underworld, Leo conceded it was a blessing in disguise, a chance to get at his own targets from a different angle. The abduction itself was initially labelled a blockheaded miscalculation, up until the girl uttered her father's name to gain leverage. As it turned out, Dvorkin had wronged a number of people in one of the money-laundering crime rings, getting his already wealthy hand caught in the cookie jar, and making arrangements to defect westward with the riches. That kind of greed was frowned upon, especially from a simpleton cobbler as himself, who had not earned his battle scars or paid necessary dues to the organization. He would reunite with his daughter, but not before an entertaining game of hide-and-seek was played.

Leo spared his niece the technicalities, for he could spin the story any way he pleased, and although he liked being a hero in her eyes, there were more important proceedings at stake.

He did love her spunk and marvelled at the precocious streak of malice she exhibited on the night of Bandura's gruesome, yet oh-so-spectacular slaughter, a memory he revived frequently like a proud parent revelling in his offspring's praiseworthy know-how. At the outset, he was unsure the actual kill was hers, though soon formulated it had to be, for there was a lack of offenders to pin it on, and no one quite so capable. With no official order on Bandura's head, Leo was left with a short list of civilian suspects, and taking into account their required proximity to the crime scene, those numbers dwindled significantly to two.

The first, Yakov Feldblum, was a wimpy Jew incapable of murder and ignorant to Bandura's insatiable hunger for young form. Had he known what the pervert was doing to his sister, he would not be up to the task still. The second, Lady Rama, could pass for a jealous lover thrown into a fit of madness, were she not already acquainted with his distorted malady, choosing to continue her affair with the lad just the same. Leo considered to have underestimated them both, granted Dessa's participation was nonsensical otherwise, and so he came to terms with the wild idea of his then eleven-year-old niece as the true perpetrator of Bandura's demise.

The challenge was not to dwell on Dessa's motives, because conceptualizing the nature of her relationship with the creep encouraged Leo to slice him over and over again. He wanted to be of help, knowing she was too smart to leave the body as is and would return before the city congested with people. As a rule, killing was the easy part, but how could a little girl muster enough stamina to singlehandedly rid of a corpse she barely had the strength to lug in the basement?

Intrigued, Leo opted to give it a day before taking matters into his own hands. He would come back the following night and dispose of the body himself, had it rested untouched. And untouched it was, with the exception of negligible bite marks peppering the skin. He worked to gain insight into Dessa's psyche and, reviewing the punctures, surmised she was counting on the rats to dissolve the corpse, a callow strategy that exposed her for the child she very much was, in spite of her murderous triumph. The notion fashioned a cursory laugh, yet her botched undertaking now called for professional clean up, and Leo was primed to dust off the old, trusty panic bag.

The panic bag encompassed an ensemble of tools paramount to disposing of unwanted human capital in a proficient, untraceable and, for the greater part, timely manner. A running joke equated them to standard issue party favours given to rookies when joining the ranks, but every member had his preferential method, and the contents of no two bags were alike.

It was on his way back to the basement that Leo spotted a woman at the far end of the street. Her stride was one he knew

180

intimately. Dropping off the bag, he came up for a second look. It was, indeed, Rama, the last person he expected to see.

The duo was well acquainted, having had an affair years ago, long ahead of the love dungeon she chose to build, thereby crossing into a morally repugnant territory of no return. In a relatively short while, Leo could not go two steps without confronting a man who had not made good use of her flesh. The style and frequency with which she was passed around made his insides churn, for the woman he once loved had turned into a moonlighting tramp, a common whore with an uncommon knack. Barring the novelty, she was no different from the hussies Leo routinely encountered in his noxious, part-time employment.

There she stood, with her precious lover dead as a doorknob beneath their feet, and he was not about to let her prance off scot-free. He reduced Rama to a liability, and whatever feelings he bore were locked away in a previous decade neither of them sustained the power to access. Marked for death anyhow, Leo submerged himself in a state of delirious, euphoric abandon, blasé to the final count of bodies he was to scrap.

In the basement, he hacked at the corpse whilst his female accomplice cowered below a grimy wall. Part of him felt sorry for her. Rama remained a known woman, an older woman, his carnal teacher, and a tender one at that; but there was not a shred of room for nostalgia, and he threw Bandura's body parts into the bags her trembling hands held out for him. They tallied fifteen in total, stacked neatly by Rama at the edge of the bloody tarp, the smell of which had mixed with the simmering stench of garbage, making for an outrageously disagreeable olfactory cocktail of putrefaction.

Playing butcher was really an appetizer for the main course of transportation and disposal. Leo's chopping demonstration alone made Rama green, so it was in his best interest to temporarily withhold the next stop on their lurid itinerary.

A voracious appetite to gamble marred the days leading up to Leo's coordinated ambush of his bosses. He made a bid to kick his debilitating fixation some time ago when he split from his then-lover, Natasha. The two of them had quite a jolly go at it, a glamorous run of nightly soirees with uninterrupted flow of champagne, tobacco, money, and cards. It was an insatiable habit he knew would thoroughly ruin him, and Nat was poison, inciting him sweetly toward annihilation.

Were Leo to survive it, he had to quit her in conjunction with the action itself, though his vanishing act was by no means for long. Gambling dens called on him. Cards seduced him. There was no self-imposed limit of playing one hand, one round, or having one drink, and a courtesy sit-down inevitably lasted well into the witching hours. He never learned when to quit a good streak and was foreseeably shot by the end of the night, floundering in deficit like an amateur. Things headed south fast. Before he knew it, the tap ran dry, money was owed, he was three sheets to the wind, and unwelcome. In that miasma, there was little to do but skedaddle and tap into Shurik's brimming repository of artefacts to work out the debt without falling casualty to the hard-boiled black suits.

With rigorous care, Leo timed his offensive to transpire in the midst of the family's out-of-town wooing of a Yank he had yet to meet. Technically equipped and mentally alert, he carried minimal optimism as to the strike's long-term outcome. An insignificant battle in a bottomless pit of a war, its momentary success was basic, but was it practical?

Leo squandered months rifling through his head for a tangibly satisfying motive, seeing as his plan was only a touch off from evolving into a uniformly successful suicide mission. Left wanting, he chalked up his rationale to occupying an existence of sensory isolation, so much so that proximate mortality rendered him unmoved. Death bored him, as did life, and he was desperate for a spark, undaunted by its potentially fatal consequences.

Were he to check out prematurely, Leo afforded himself the license to satiate his impulses an extra night as a resigning alcoholic would with a ceremonial drink or a smoker with a token cigarette. He was unconvinced by the idea of quitting cold, for even quitting commanded a hint of pleasure to help stimulate the cloying nostalgia of vices past.

Leo was well versed in the strangeness of life, with every cloaked stretch retaining behind it a tantalizing promise of everything and nothing, be it a fateful break or more of the same blaring nullity. Whenever bad habits were gratified for a last time, nature's unwritten law stipulated a tragic price for its subject's lack of willpower. Leading up to it were ominous feelings advocating restraint at all cost, and humans recurrently ignored their intuition in life's critical junctures. The inner voice they energetically tuned into on a daily basis for the most trivial of things was the same voice they willingly slighted in matters of importance.

Leo followed suit. His gut was adamant about retiring early and using the spare hours to read a book, play an aria, or surf the telly, to do anything but go out. Like many, he lived for the thrill of testing fate, accepting its omens as challenges instead of warnings. No one he knew in the flesh ever lived to tell the tale. It was always a friend of a friend who had cheated death, someone beyond borders, unreachable, untraceable, a legend with no physical presence as proof.

No matter. He left the safety of his apartment and headed to a gambling den several blocks over.

It was New Year's Eve.

"Leo," his insides droned prophetically, "is the die cast, must at this one throw all thou hast gained be lost?"

He marched on, because man was stubbornly foolhardy.

Gaining entry mirrored a funeral procession as Leo descended into an exaggerated tunnel of imposing barrelled ceilings and heavy velvet draperies, the light at the end of which he could not see.

The suits anticipated his coming; their arrangement was pre-set. Leo interrogated himself about a veiled tipoff. The den had no explicit connection to his branch, nor was it part of a different division feuding with his own, making their incentive and timing a mystery. They knew not of his murderous plan and had to be after something of Shurik's, for Leo had less than a dime to his name and was a lousy bet for generating surplus financial gain.

On each jaunt, he vowed to cut out debt free. The opposite invariably rang true, and this night would stay faithful to his vested tradition. The cards stank from the start, far from the enjoyable nostalgia he set out to draft; and this time, after a slew of bad hands, he was guarded to get on. On a regular evening, Leo's hard luck and boozed-up maundering merited icy stares from dealers and barmen much acquainted with his vacillating fortuity. This night, every man on the floor worked to preserve his company. The drinks and small talk kept coming, as did the cards and the debt. His vision blurred and knees weakened; he was getting drunk exceedingly fast. Within an hour of dropping anchor, he keeled over in his bar stool.

When Leo came to, he guessed he was still in the den, in a concealed part not for the meddling eyes and ears of the general public. It was a grungy old room, with a commendable ambiance of terror, a place where knees were broken, arms twisted, teeth pulled, and heads shot through and through. He was tied to a splintered Windsor chair, above him a flimsy chain with a light bulb faintly swinging from a draft, the direction of which he could not quite pinpoint. Sooner or later, the door he faced was bound to open, and somebody, by all odds a male representative, would set foot inside for a friendly tête-à-tête.

Until then, Leo took bets with himself as to the identity of this stranger, determining it to be a surprise every which way.

The climax of his self-centred film was unravelling, with the major plot twist upon him, or would it be a red herring? There was nothing to gain from his capture. If they wanted him dead, he would be peacefully resting six feet under. Despite his evasive nature and a talent for lying low, no one survived an upward of six months of freedom with a bounty on their head.

Not fond of theatrics, Leo wanted to get the show over, and though his hands were tied, his mouth was gag free, so he stomped his feet and yelled for someone to come near. The existing silence taunted him, and he went on hollering. Multiple sets of footsteps echoed around his enclosure, the doorknob jerked, and a pudgy figure waddled in. The man converged on him, stabilizing the swinging light bulb above their heads.

"Hello, brother," he said.

Leo squinted, jogging his memory to no advantage.

"I'm afraid we don't know each other well enough for you to address me as brother."

"My apologies, Leonid. I suppose you don't remember me."

"Correct."

"You do, however, remember Natasha? And fondly, I hope."

"Don't tell me you are her crazed father."

"Nothing so noble, though I am her husband."

Leo was in stitches. "Well, of course, you are. How unpredictably predictable. I must sincerely apologize. I had no idea."

"None of them did, my friend."

Leo's giggles subsided. He was unsure of what bothered him more, the plural form of other men, or the past tense of their knowing her.

"Don't get me wrong, you're a fancy fella," the man simpered, "but you aren't the baddest rooster in the coop."

"Right. And now you've cooked up a hearty stew of revenge?"

"Don't flatter yourself. There are no hard feelings from either of us. She had a good time. I'll give you that. You have a special flair in wooing women on someone else's dime."

"How shall I be of service, then?"

"You have a selection of items we are interested in. To be clear, they aren't effectively yours. Nothing is yours, for you haven't earned it, nor do you deserve to inherit it."

"If it's items you wanted, you could've robbed the place at your discretion with no need for me or my endorsement."

"Your father is in possession of an article worth more than all his treasures combined. Natasha never found it on the surface, and that's where you shall be of service."

"Father hides things, first and foremost, from me."

"It hasn't deterred you from ransacking the place, anyhow."

"Look, if you want something, it's yours, but count me out of the treasure hunt. I hold no key."

"We aren't negotiating. You're coming."

"And my debt?"

"What of it?"

"Will it cancel itself out with my due cooperation?"

"The debt isn't with me. It's with the den."

"Your den."

"Not even remotely."

"Those goons drugged me. I could've made good."

"You seldom do, Leonid, and if you did, where's the fun in that? You walk the walk and talk the talk of an aristocrat, half-arsing your generous employment with a 'my shit smells of roses' perma-grin. Are you under the false impression that your education holds you to a higher moral standard than us déclassé cutthroats?"

"I am under no impressions, Mister—?"

"When you wake up tomorrow, if you choose to, that is, you

186

will have fallen far and hard from the pedestal you so eloquently erected for yourself."

"Sounds like a great setup you've got brewing."

"You set yourself up when you decided to wear your big boy pants in this business. Truth is, you aren't cut out for it, nor will you be. I give you ten minutes to make your payment arrangements with the house."

The man bailed out, leaving the door unshut. Leo was tellingly panicked, his plans considerably shot to hell. This was a spark, all right. Shurik's theatre chandelier and Venetian mirrors were topnotch, but they were in plain sight, and Nat was looking for an invisible cash cow. Were the heirlooms to be smuggled to Western Europe or stateside, they could fetch upward a million to a decorous collector, and what artefact was possibly more advantageous than that?

A new man peeked in and, by the looks of it, was the newly minted owner of the house.

"You must be the debt collector. What do I owe?"

The man chuckled without supplying an answer.

"I'd like a number, please."

"Would you also like a smoke to go with that number?" the man asked, lighting a cigarette and extending it to Leo, who pursed his lips and took a lengthy drag.

"I'll take everything they don't."

"Excuse me?"

Leo's attention was called to the tight hallway where Nat's husband conversed with his henchmen.

"I'd rather you give me a fair number."

"You'll be lucky if we don't hang you by the end of the night, you piece of shit. Here, let me put that out for you."

He took the cigarette and drove it into Leo's left cheek.

"Welcome to the killing fields, angel face."

Chapter 22

Leo rode in the back of a pristinely kept '74 ZIL-115. Lodged shoulder to shoulder between two portly, balding clods, he sank into the welcoming luxury of the leather seat. The car glided over cobblestone roads with spellbinding ease, and the smoothness of the ride lulled him into passivity. Through heavily tinted windows, he made out the usual neighbourhood markers. Streletzkaya Street was not far off. This was happening. No amount of wishing it away, rubbing his eyes, or pinching himself could delay the inevitable.

They rolled past Leo's building and turned into its courtyard where the chauffeur pulled up to the row of maintenance sheds and turned off the engine. In the passenger's seat, Nat's husband excitedly kneaded his palms.

"Shall we?" he lisped, wiggling himself sideways.

Pudgy, thought Leo. He would name this caricature, Pudgy.

A second ZIL-115 braked behind them. It was the new den owner. The pit boss. The Pit Bull. He came on them, knocked on the window, and motioned everyone to get out.

The clods exited first, then Leo. Pudgy gave inaudible orders to his stone-faced chauffeur and joined the group.

"You're the shepherd, Faustov!" he said.

The basement tunnels led them to the ground floor where Pudgy insisted on calling the elevator.

They piled into the cage. Leo pressed "2" and leaned into the sliding doors.

۞

Pit Bull's associates joined the mammoth larceny within minutes, having parked a UAZ Bukhanka van near the basement entrance to transport the loot.

Shurik's Venetian mirrors were loaded first. Stacks of special library editions went next. Pudgy's clods were boxing sets of fine china and silver service. The operation demonstrated impressive efficiency, with bandits rotating like clockwork between the flat and their van.

Leo sat dejected in a corner of the dining room. By all accounts, Pudgy truly was seeking something else, an item not for personal gain, but one he owed or was sent to find for another wanting party. As the flat emptied, he grew restless.

"Keep at it!" he barked. "Search every drawer, every crevice."

"Whatever you're looking for clearly isn't here," said Leo at last.

"I'm not leaving without it, you little shit."

"It? What is it? Humour me, Pudgy."

"The Safari, you arse! I want the Safari!"

Leo was shaken out of his lethargic indifference. Dessa's Safari.

"All done here," Pit Bull interrupted. "Don't ever set foot on my floor again, angel face. You play; you pay. And, by the look of things, this isn't your most auspicious pastime." He saluted the room and disappeared.

Leo felt a cold, weighted blade settle near his throat.

"Do it already," he pleaded.

"I will, if you don't give me what I want."

"You will, regardless of what I give you."

"Yes, but instead of leaving empty-handed, I will sit in this very corner and wait for your father, your sister, and your niece. Believe me, you'll have gotten off easy by the time I'm through with them."

"It's in the upstairs flat. I'll go get it."

"Just like that! He'll go get it!" Pudgy joked.

He struck Leo with the hilt of his dagger as the clods lifted him up by the collar of his Chesterfield. They barrelled out of Shurik's apartment, called on the elevator, and headed upward.

Inside, Leo shot straight for Dessa's bedroom. He paced about, scanning the area. Not in plain view. Not in her closet, the dresser, or the desk. Not on the shelves. He reached under the bed and felt for her jewellery box.

"Bingo!" snorted Pudgy when Leo unwrapped the figurines. "Bring them here."

He snatched half, leaving Leo to carry the rest, and waddled into the kitchen where his clods readily waited.

"Sit down," he said, gingerly sorting the porcelain animals on a round glass tray. He leaned into Leo and shook a figurine close to his ear. "Hear that?"

"Barely."

"Listen carefully."

"Sand?" guessed Leo.

"Magic sand."

One of the clods handed Pudgy a pair of brass walnut pliers.

"It's not what's on the outside, Leo," he said.

Taking the African lion, he squeezed the pliers, the porcelain head cracked open, and a stream of granules formed a convincing mound in the centre of the platter. It shined with large nuggets of precious gemstones. "Like a Kinder Surprise for grown-ups."

"They're all filled with diamonds?"

190

"Diamonds, rubies, garnets. And not just any ol' rocks! These here are from Tsarist regalia, and nearly priceless."

"My bet was drugs."

"Come now, Faustov. Don't be so pedestrian."

"And Bandura sniffed them out?"

"You see, our Pedo errand boy got his hand stuck in the honey pot. Not all of the porcelain sets are alike in content, and the kid got lucky when we had an unfortunate leak of information. Some are filled with your run-of-the-mill nose powder, of course. Others hold gems, or gold, but their value is insignificant in the great scheme of things. This set; these gemstones are not about money. This is power. Authority. Control. So, the kid decided to combine our business with his twisted pleasures, pawning these off one by one to your girl, but knowing exactly where they were, had he ever needed them. Until he got dead, that is."

"How do you know?"

"Well, he certainly didn't make off with the spoils, did he?"

"You knew she had them."

"No, I thought you had them and she was a mere transport of goods between you and the errand boy. I still think it, and it's rather cowardly to keep your stash here, no? Such high risk, even if they were filled with cheap fairy dust."

"You're wrong."

"You've been adamant about that. Yet, here we sit."

Leo got up to leave.

"We're not done," echoed Pudgy.

"You found what you needed."

"Yes, and now we're going to take a very long ride."

"A ride?"

"To the Kaniv Reservoir."

Leo flinched. He knew it well. One hundred and sixty kilometres of water surrounded by thick forests every which way.

No one ever went in to come out alive. He stretched for the hunting knife strapped to his right ankle. It was too late. The clods pounced on him in seconds as he bucked and clawed to get free. A blow to the head, and the ground shifted beneath him. This was it, he thought.

This was really it.

Chapter 23

Prior to following through with a call to the police, Dessa raced past Chuck into her room. The costliest antiques, her chifforobe, fauteuil, and secretary, were exactly as she left them. Diving under her bed, she removed the jewellery box containing her prized porcelain figurines. The collection was gone, its filler of crinkled tissue paper and velvet scraps strewn about as a dour reminder. Because of its free, morally tainted acquisition and lack of importance beyond cosmetic appeal, there was no need for the girl to mourn its loss, nor did she, as new questions arose with each fading second. Why were the main rarities in her room intact, and were Mother's riches similarly disposed of?

Of greater significance, the collection's glaring disappearance categorically established Uncle Leo as a perpetrator in the robbery downstairs. Aside from Dessa, he was the only living person to know of its unprincipled origins and plush value. She wound back to their conclusive bedtime conference in November, eliciting her courageous professions to give up any and all material things in exchange for Inna's security. A "liberal offer," he called it, and this was a fire sale under extreme duress. Singling out the figurines alluded to a cryptic message from him to her, one she could not grapple with submerged neck-deep in pandemonium.

For Inna to cost even half the king's ransom irreplaceably purloined from the Faustov dynasty seemed absurd; and had she, Dessa was sceptical her return at this monumental expense was justified. Uncle Leo was right in that they were not good friends, and to financially ruin their own family for the brat of a petty desperado was a juvenile, thankless idea.

Noting the yet-unplaced call to police headquarters, she moved out into the hallway where Chuck patrolled the foyer, impatiently tapping his feet, unsure of the role he was to assume in this mess.

When Mother barged in, outwardly hysterical and bellowing with rage, Dessa was quick to reach for the telephone.

"No!" she said. "No police!"

Chuck deciphered that much in her shrieks and was intent on obtaining a sufficing clarification for her change of heart. Mother repeated herself emphatically in broken English, for she, too, was now privy to the culprit's identity.

"This is family problem, we must solve ourselves," she reiterated and took off in the direction of her bedroom, no doubt to check on the safety of her own belongings.

By and by, she came out in mollified form, her hysteria slowly subsiding. With Mother's riches evidently uncompromised, Dessa withheld her case of unaccounted-for figurines, as the woman knew nothing of them, and their abrupt disclosure would prompt an exasperating inquisition.

"I must find your uncle at once," she said, hunching for her phonebook and unplugging the telephone.

"And Grandpapa?"

"I'll make the calls from there. You two stay put."

She went off, leaving them to their own devices. Chuck was growing incessantly confused.

194

"Uncle Leo is responsible," Dessa said.

"He robbed his father?"

"He had to, or he thought he did. He was saving somebody, you see, or he thought he was."

Chuck shook his head.

"I can't explain it any further. Please, excuse me."

She started back to her room on the off chance that a note from Klara awaited; it did. Having sat there for days, maybe weeks, Dessa eagerly ripped into it to confirm her suspicions.

Dear Dessa,

I am writing on December 20th. The breaking news is this: In recent days, Inna has been handed over to her father unscathed. I don't know the fine points, only what was filtered down to me from Yakov. He said that, luckily, your uncle didn't have to lift a finger in the matter.

Inna is not returning to the academy and will flee to Hungary with her family before the New Year's. She leaves no forwarding address, and I lack faith we will see her again. Are you getting on with your guest?–Klara

A single line held Dessa's concentration, its ramifications positively devastating if found to be rooted in truth. Were Inna's release not the driving force behind Uncle's thievery, nothing short of atrocious personal greed or cowardice would goad him to launch the colossal sweep.

In later hours of the evening, Chuck found his niche as comforter of Mother, who was uninspired to relay the success rate of her calls in tracking Leo and dismissed Dessa to her room early so as to not interfere with the couple's bonding.

The girl had a hard time believing her uncle would dare submit himself at all, much less so soon, but when the grown-ups were visibly distracted, convinced she was fast asleep, Dessa ditched the warmth of her bed in favour of staking out Shurik's flat to catch sight of Leo, were he to show.

The drastic state of family affairs had thrown Mother's rigorously crafted plans of forthcoming marital bliss and emigration into disarray. The riches she was banking on to look less desperate and more desirable were expertly nullified. Were there a proposal, to accept it after having lost the upper hand among a passel of young brides in waiting would be the ultimate gesture of desperation. The ripples of Leo's shopping spree were pervasive, ranging far beyond basic commercial deficit. Mother dreamt for their names to be forever disassociated. Like a junkie on his last fix or a drunkard dozing at the wheel, she prayed for her brother to perish, to face a speeding trolley, or get caught in a crossfire between his own belligerents, for he was an infectious, incurable cancer and better off dead.

To Mother's surprise, a marriage proposal came within two days of Chuck's departure. Having seen the damages first hand, he forecast the offer would make her feel ill at ease. This was a woman too proud for handouts, and a charity case she was not; an answer exclusive of a firm "no" resembled a fantasy. He wanted her as his wife. He would extend an invitation to Shurik, if need be. He had to try, because he wanted Dessa the most.

His proposal was accepted, though Mother talked of just the two of them, insistent Dessa's schooling was to be carried out in the homeland. Shurik was up to the task of assuming legal guardianship if asked, and in case of emergency, the care of distant relatives and faithful friends would not fail her. In any event, a permanent move for the girl was non-negotiable.

Not sold on the idea, Chuck demanded, believing he was in a position to do so unhindered, that Dessa come with. Had Shurik chosen to stay put, he could visit them in America at his leisure, but the marriage offer was contingent on the girl's imminent adoption as his own. Faced with an ultimatum to leave as a trio or not at all, Mother dissolved into submission after a laudable show of resistance.

The moment of his homecoming, Chuck got on the paperwork, drafting a formal invitation for the girl and her mother to join him, wording it as a curtailed visit and not a permanent move, as the latter was legally forbidden by their law. Expedited, an approval could come within months, allowing him to fly back as early as springtime to take them away.

୨▲

The heart of winter loomed, Leo's whereabouts continued to puzzle, and neither Mother nor Shurik were up for discussing it. A stream of intentional amnesia drifted in and out of their everyday lives, the trauma so abysmal, it had to be stowed deep in the attic of their subconscious. Dessa found the dead air indicative of compliance with a budding belief that Leo would not return of his own volition. His activity and condition unknown, the family prepared themselves for the worst. On some nights, they may have preferred it.

It was in the last days of February, after braving a harsh blizzard on her way home from school, that Dessa eavesdropped on a pair of hoarse voices as she trekked up the winding staircase to her apartment. The wait was over. Leo materialized.

A door fastened shut as she stepped foot onto Shurik's floor. The voices lingered in his corridor where he and Leo launched into a heated argument, and rightfully so.

From bits and pieces of their broken dialogue, Dessa pasted together an ugly picture of events leading up to and including the break-in. Uncle Leo was a world-class poltroon, a liar who used Inna as a front to pay off yet another mound of gambling debts gone wrong. Having been previously tipped off to her uninjured return, he needed not do a thing about it.

For a cold, cunning deceiver, Leo was strangely apologetic. He spoke of compromised operations yielding debts at once recent and past, debts he was jointly held accountable for one night without proper notice or a fair trial. Dessa entertained the idea that her found address book was his all along.

Leo's fading words were those of ruthless men, dark trunks, deep waters, forsaken woods, and systematic torture.

"They were going to hang me from that very tree, Father," wept the charlatan, presumably on his knees.

Detaching herself from their verbal battle royal, the girl started off, longing for the comfort of her dusky quarters and the enveloping softness of her cotton sheets.

"And so they should have," she spit through her teeth, turning onto the stairway, "for no one gives a toss about rats."

Chapter 24

Mid-spring, Mother got word from Chuck of their cleared paperwork. The invitations were granted without a hitch, and he was to fly out at his earliest convenience, instructed to keep mum around Dessa on the length of their upcoming stay. Mother convinced him it had to be a surprise revealed well after departure, for the girl grew comfortable in her surroundings and was far too sensitive to adequately process the permanency of their move. Reluctantly, he agreed to her terms.

Advised of Chuck's encore stopover, Dessa was delirious with bliss. It was his turn to play host and open to them an exotic world they had only ever glimpsed on the telly. She pictured an idyllic summer like none before it, teeming with brand-new memories, untrodden paths, and youthful discoveries to be recounted amongst friends upon her faithful return. These adventures guaranteed her a loftier position in the upper echelons of student affairs, artfully diverting focus from rumours of her family's bygone riches to the glamorous exclusivity of foreign marriage and transatlantic voyages.

She started a packing itinerary weeks prior to Chuck's arrival, the contents of her valise changing on the hour. While Mother insisted on Dessa packing light, her own luggage grew exponentially, holding jewels, family albums, several sets of fine china, and seasonal clothing, including her enviable collection of furs.

కా

On the Sunday of May 9th, 1993, Dessa skipped the stately Victory Day Parade in favour of a much-delayed visit to her dear Papa Carlo. The family trip was scheduled for the following afternoon, and this was her last opportunity to arrange their fond adieus. He, too, was a veteran, and she proudly carried with her a hand-painted card and a bouquet of bright red tulips and Gerbera daisies.

Although closed for business, the old man was in his shop testing a new addition to his magical warehouse, a glorious Bechstein grand piano. The concert pianists often pontificated that everything sounded better on a Bechstein, and on this day, watching him light up at the keys with a handful of simple folk jingles, Dessa could not agree more. The essence of gaiety, of human affection, and its innumerable capacity when summoned upon, lingered in every note, every breath, every cheer, and it was beautiful.

Papa Carlo made a strong brew of Russian Caravan in his antique silver samovar. Dessa was treated to a plate of biscotti, raspberry jam, and chocolates. When he talked, she listened. When she talked, he listened. They took turns reading Pushkin's The Tale of the Priest and of his Workman Balda, exchanging impressions in words, in laughter, and in complementary silence.

కా

Standing in line for a beef pasty on her way home, Dessa witnessed an elderly woman faint next to the vendor's cart. Meddlesome persons gathered round, fanning her head, poking at her like roadkill with their shoes and umbrellas. Dessa noted a half-eaten meat pie next to the body. The woman foamed at the mouth as onlookers pointed fingers and raised their voices at the young vendor.

"Poisoned! She was poisoned," they hollered, throwing their own purchases in rubbish bins and demanding refunds. Others lifted their arms high to the bright blue sky calling for divine intervention.

The woman was slipping away, her extremities turning a dusty hue of olive drab. Something about this contrasting scene was delectably sinister, and Dessa kept watch, soaking in the mounting dread and helplessness of death until a pair of glassy-eyed medics sluggishly loaded her pallid carcass into an ambulance.

Dessa circled the streets of her neighbourhood and beyond, spurning all thoughts of home. At present, their flat had a feeling of an oversized storage unit. Everything, including their memories, was wrapped, boxed, taped, locked, and stacked for extraction. People dropped in and out every day for the past week, professing their heartfelt goodbyes and wishes of good fortune for the future. If she never had to see these prattling gossip hounds again, the world would be better for it. The busybodies knew more than they let on, for they were too saccharine in their farewells with Dessa, but carried on with Mother in an assortment of sombre stares, lowered voices, and clinched fists. They were saying goodbye in the truest sense of the word.

Mother and Chuck were at the parade with Shurik and would be out for hours. A stack of passports, itineraries, and boarding passes towered on the kitchen table. They would sit around it tomorrow morning and observe a few minutes of silence, a cultural custom encouraging luck and welfare for travellers prior to departure. The first set of passes would take them to Warsaw for a week long stay to sort out more paperwork. If all went well, the second set would take them to America.

Upon coming home, she called Klara. Dessa lounged on the pyramid of luggage in the foyer, reciting to Klara her memories of the day. It was imperative for them to talk, to reminisce, to remind each other of the great times they had, but those were further in the past than she imagined, and recent events were nothing to get nostalgic about. Sitting in silence, the girls engaged in a game they often played when alone, a game of staying on the line the longest; a game Dessa usually won.

"You'll be gone like Inna," Klara spoke.

"Silly girl. It's just for the summer. I promise to write weekly," replied Dessa with more than a little trepidation, suddenly petrified at the notion of not seeing each other again.

There was no response on Klara's end of the line, only a break in breathing, a sigh, an inaudible stream of tears.

Forty-five minutes slipped by them, and for the first time in a long time, Dessa hung up the receiver first.

Chapter 25

In the final hours of the night's ritual packing, unpacking, and spirited send-offs, Uncle Leo dropped in for an unwelcome appearance.

From her room, Dessa made out his voice in the foyer, sauced to the bone and engaged in a verbal scuffle with Mother. He was staggering in the corridor, nearing her room, calling her name.

"There you are, sport," he said, barging into her room.

"Leave her be!" shouted Mother, hammering him with her fists as he shouldered her backwards, reclining on the closed door. She pounded on it and rattled a telephone receiver as if to call the police, a threat all three of them knew was empty.

"Give her a second, she'll smarten up and run to get your grandpapa, giving us a window of quietude," Uncle Leo said.

The banging ceased, and Mother took off downstairs. Leo wiggled his brows with satisfaction.

"You are a filthy liar and a thief to boot," Dessa said without looking up from her secretary.

"And you are a wee murderess, my dear, having caused me great peril. Yet, I was never so crass as to greet you in disdainful fashion."

"Why are you here?"

"I came to say, Bon Voyage."

"Are you leaving?"

"Looks like we both are."

"Alright then, best of luck." She tapped her fingers, supposing it as good a time as any for a reveal of her own. "I did take that hussy's watch, by the way."

"Lived well on it, did you?"

"The rats in the sewer may have."

"You dropped it in a sewer? Are you mad? Have you the slightest idea how much it was worth?"

"Not a dime. To me, that is. The value of things, of people even, it's quite subjective. Isn't it, Uncle?"

"Your thumb-sucking friend was returned in one piece, was she not?"

"And don't for a moment pretend it was on account of your good graces with those cons, either. You're a small-timer. You did nothing except fool me long enough into thinking otherwise."

She refused to meet his line of sight, so he tottered through the thick, caustic air, pinched her cheek, and turned on his heel.

"Aren't you forgetting something?" she asked.

When he looked back, the savannah elephant towered in the tiny palm of her hand.

"My God, Dessa."

"Surprised?"

"I—"

"You're the one who left it for me."

"Yes, but—

"It saved you."

"What?"

"The missing piece saved you. I carry it everywhere. One day, it chipped. You can imagine my surprise when further inspection yielded a handful of sumptuous rubies. I glued it back together."

204

"Rubies?"

"Yes, like late Grandmamma's."

"No, Dessa, not like Grandmamma's."

"You didn't know it, until the person you gave it to realized one figurine was missing. That's why they let you go. The promise of finding it."

"They didn't let me go."

"Doesn't much matter to me how or why you are here."

"I need a favour from you, sport."

He stooped in front of her and cupped her elbows.

"You can have it," she said.

"No, that's not it, kiddo. I need you to hold on to it for me. Take it with you. Wrap it up nice and tight and take it with you. Can you do that for your old, wretched uncle?"

"And when I get back?"

He tickled her knees and straightened his posture.

"We'll cross that bridge when we come to it. It goes without saying, not a word of it to Mother."

"That's obvious."

"Then we have a deal?"

"If you answer me one."

"Shoot."

"What did you do with it?" she asked. "The body."

"Which part?" he grinned.

She thought him crazed. A blink of villainy washed over his weathered features. There was comfort in it, in that rare quality best described as an inexhaustible capacity for cruelness. She had it, too.

"Have you sworn yourself to secrecy, Uncle?"

"You know what they say: the only way for two people to keep a secret is–"

"–If one of them is dead."

He nodded, suddenly uncomfortable and rash.

205

"That reminds me, I've got another drop-in to make."

"Wait! In your address book, there was an address we couldn't solve, the very last one by the tattered spine."

"It's where I'll be, sport!" he echoed from the hall.

"But, it doesn't exist."

"That's the appeal!"

At a quarter to midnight, Rama's doorbell rang. It was Leo.

"I need to crash here for the night, no strings."

"Can't tonight, I've got company, Leo."

"I'm not asking. Get rid of him," he said, proceeding inside without consent. "I'll be in your study."

Rama sped down the corridor into her client room. Ten minutes later, hustled footsteps glided along the floorboards, their heaviness vibrating across surfaces high and low before a body exited the apartment. They were alone.

She joined him. "They'll find you, if you stay."

"You've assumed awful quickly they're bothering to look. Yet, here I am."

"Yes. Don't take offense, but how is it that you are?"

"Knowledge is a powerful tool in keeping others from skinning your hide."

"Cowardice works wonders, too."

"That it does, old girl, though self-preservation has a more forgiving ring to it."

"What possible knowledge can hold their interest after you let them strip the place clean?"

"Now there's a bedtime story. For another night, perhaps."

"What happened to you at the reservoir?"

"Does it matter?"

"You showed up on my doorstep beaten, bloodied, white as a sheet, and soaked to the bone. In December, no less!"

"I swam home."

"Stop it. I heard you killed Nat's husband."

"Pudgy? Nah. Another dunce I can't take full credit for."

"If it wasn't you–"

"A misunderstanding. Everyone's got a boss, even ol' Pudgy. He had a delivery to make before putting me six feet under, and it so happened some of the order went missing."

"In transit?"

"No, from the start. He should've checked, should've known better, but, for my sake, he was every bit the dope I worked him out to be. In a war of wits, I'll win every time. All I had to do was convincingly shift the blame onto the fatso, and he was toast."

"So you struck a deal with his boss?"

"Sure."

"Sounds too simple."

"I may be fibbing a little."

"A little?"

"Or, a lot. Let it rest, old girl."

"I'm not working for them like you think I am, Leo."

"You're not working for them like you think you are, either. Can't you see, behind every gate there stand ten more, and we will never know the depth of the labyrinth."

"Nor should we. Live and let live."

"We don't know how to live. Have you tasted air beyond these stale walls? We've been given a chance to break free, to go anywhere and see anything, to live like real people, normal people. This here is a glorified swamp."

"I like the swamp."

"You always have."

"It has its comforts."

"And your nightmares? Have they ceased?"

"Savagery doesn't cease."

"You're a strange one, Rama. With everything you're willing to do in that love dungeon, that is what bothers you?"

"No, what bothers me is that, to this very day, it hasn't bothered you."

"Why should it? The human body makes for great fertilizer, though I've a sneaking suspicion you haven't eyed a plate of your favourite ham croquettes ever since that earsplitting, rusted grinder broke down on us," he snorted.

"You're ill."

"I feel fine, actually. A tad dotty, maybe."

"Psychopathic. I'm heading to bed."

"Before you go, will you do me a kindness?"

She listened.

"Keep near Father for me. My sister is about to make a run for it with a Yank and is taking the chicklet with her."

"When are they coming back?"

"They aren't."

"Dessa hasn't talked about it in those terms."

"She doesn't think it's permanent."

"She isn't stupid, she must know."

"Selective naiveté has its comforts," he frowned.

"Alright. I'll keep watch."

The doorbell sounded.

"A client this late?"

"No. I've no idea who it is."

"Let me get it, then. Sit tight."

He went to the door.

A wheezing, heavyset man was diligently wiping his shoes on the welcome mat.

"Is Lady Ramazanova in?"

"And you are?"

"Detective Komarovsky."

Leo knew the name.

"Is there an emergency, detective?"

"Not that I know of."

208

"Then it's a rather bizarre time for house calls, wouldn't you agree?"

"I do apologize; this is unofficial, off the clock."

"Oh, I understand," he winked, wondering just how deep the rabbit hole went.

"Let him in," Rama said, peeking from the study.

Leo nudged his way out of the flat.

"I thought you were staying the night."

"No, old girl. It's best I don't."

Komarovsky kept Leo in his sights, struck with a fluky vibe of familiarity.

"I'm sorry, have we met? You look–"

"Not likely," Leo countered and headed for the stairs full tilt, popping the collar of his dinner jacket.

The detective galumphed into Rama's tight foyer.

"How may I be of service?" she asked, keeping her distance.

"I was passing through. On, er– on my way home. You know, the precinct, it's–"

"Conveniently close, yes."

"Yes," he grunted.

"Within an arm's reach when you don't need it and a hair too far when you do," reflected her voice to no one in particular.

He shuffled his feet, picking at his fingernails.

"I was told my visit would not appear unmannerly, as these are your working hours."

Bewildered, she emerged from her study.

"You're here on recommendation? I'm sorry, I can't take on new clients, especially you."

"That's not at all what I meant!" he jumped, stupefied at her incoherence. "I've come to tell you we've sealed the case on Sasha Bandura. Officially, that is."

"Solved?"

"Unsolved."

"A year later and still unsolved, hmm?"

"Almost to the week, in fact. A bit surprising you'd remember." He eyed the darkness of her interiors. "Or not."

"If there's something you're itching to ask, then ask. It's late, and I've no enthusiasm for your riddles."

"I want the truth. Case is closed, what you say stays off record. No harm, no foul. I wasn't here, and we never spoke."

"Except you were, we did, and you've got a friend who has knowledge of your whereabouts – and mine."

"Bandura may not have vanished at your hands, Lady Ramazanova, but you certainly took part in keeping him so."

"Proof?"

"Hunch."

"Unreliable."

"Never wrong."

"Mister Komarovsky," she laughed, motioning him out the door, "you operate within a profiteering system where rock-solid evidence is subject to, shall we say, financial currents. Right or wrong, hunch or no hunch, doesn't really come into it so long as those winds blow on target."

"I beg your pardon?"

"You know as well as I do, a fresh stack of rubles, or dollars, whatever your poison, can yield a new interpretation of any case, its motives and, above all, its suspects."

Komarovsky ogled the vacant staircase, reminded of his missed acquaintance.

"Who was that man?"

"An interpretation you've been aimlessly searching for, detective. And now a ghost, goodnight."

The door latched. The familiar stranger, having bounced around the shadows and into the night, was not to be seen again.